Peter Hollywood was born in Newry, Co. Down, in 1959. He has worked in a variety of jobs including bookselling and teaching. He has previously published two collections *Jane Alley* (Pretani Press, 1987) and *Lead City & Other Stories* (Lagan Press, 2002). He lives in Belfast with his wife and three children.

By the same author

Short Stories
Jane Alley
Lead City & Other Stories

LUGGAGE

24.04.'08

To Carol
with thanks

LUGGAGE

PETER HOLLYWOOD

LAGAN PRESS
BELFAST
2008

Published by
Lagan Press
1A Bryson Street
Belfast BT5 4ES
e-mail: lagan-press@e-books.org.uk
web: lagan-press.org.uk

ISBN (10 digit): 1 904652 43 3
ISBN (13 digit): 978 1 904652 43 4
Author: Hollywood, Peter
Title: Luggage
2008

Set in Palatino
Printed by J.H. Haynes, Sparkford

To Susan
co-pilot

*'Le corps se transforme en passant une frontière,
on le sait aussi, le regard change de focale et d'objectif,
la densité de l'air s'altère et les parfums,
les bruits se decoupent singulièrement,
jusqu'au soleil lui-même qui a une autre tête.'*
—from 'Je M'en Vais' by Jean Echenoz

'The Gascons are a sort of Ulstermen ... '
—Derek Mahon, from the introduction to his translation
of Cyrano de Bergerac, by Edmond Rostand.

LUGGAGE

One

THEIR GREEN CANOE SHOT ROUND THE bend in the river
with the sleek, green pebbles glistening and visible beneath
them on the riverbed and the river's sinews, for the moment,
pulled tight and taut and powerful. The two young boys, in the
canoe with Thomas, were gleeful and excited and they
splashed him in their excitement with their paddles. Thomas
was also wet from his own sweat and yet he had to smile at the
boys' shrill reactions.

He was having difficulty keeping to the mainstream though
and had to work his paddle hard to prevent the current carrying
them into the far riverbank. He moved his body to rock the
canoe round and with measured strokes kept the craft quite
near the middle. The manoeuvre caused some nervous yelps
from his son and older companion but these quickly passed.

— Keep an eye out for Indians, he shouted but really only to himself now for he had earlier mentioned Hurons and then Mohiccans but neither his six-year-old nor his friends' ten-year-old had got the reference, so he had now simplified matters to 'Indians.' The boys were more intent, anyway, on keeping this canoe in the lead, pursued as they were by the other two canoes, containing the rest of the two families, conjoined for the day's outing. Thomas, however, decided to slow up. They paddled into a quiet stretch and the boys lifted their paddles while Thomas let the canoe swing around and tried to hold it at right angles to the flow of the river, just outside the main stream of the current.

They looked up and saw Andrew's canoe come careening round the bend and the sun glint off his spectacles. In the bow sat Thomas's oldest girl, Laura, and, behind her, Andrew's daughter, Claire; their thin laughter could be heard despite the wind that had begun, suddenly, to blow against them. Thomas waved and promptly lost control of the canoe, which the river kicked around in a circle.

— Quick, 'crew', he shouted. We've got to get facing downstream again.

In their awkward eagerness to do this, they almost toppled and overturned. By the time they were successfully re-aligned with the flow, Thomas was out of breath and Andrew and the girls were laughing and enjoying the boys' predicament as they skimmed gleefully past them into the lead.

— Any sign of the girls? Thomas roared after them, referring to the third canoe, containing their wives and Thomas's second daughter, Molly.

Andrew played weekend rugby in Dundee and he seemed too bulky and compressed into his boat, yet his accent was a soft one and Thomas could not catch the reply. The wind was very strong now and the going not as straight forward as it had been on the earlier stretches of the river. Now Thomas seemed to have less time to look up and around him.

16

— Look. There they are, Donald pointed back the ways.

Thomas tried to keep balance and look around and saw the girls come calmly round the curve.

— Come on dad: let's get going, his son, Jason, complained. Andrew and the girls are miles away now.

So, Thomas made determined gouges at the water with his paddle.

The wind worked hard against them, stitching cross-eddies into the surface of the Dordogne. The banks on either side were overgrown with dense foliage and heavy undergrowth and here and there cliff faces glowered down at them over treetops. It was a wilder stretch of the river. They had already glided past La Roque Gageac, skating across the medieval town's reflection in the water and Thomas had let the boys paddle while he gazed up at the precipice. The troglodyte fort, hewn into the rock face, had remained impregnable during the Hundred Years War and untaken too in the subsequent sixteenth century wars of religion when the Huguenots were driven into Northern Europe.

Beneath Beynac, they had run the canoes aground on the river shoal across from where the tour buses groaned past and tourists leaned on the walls and balustrades overlooking the river. Here they had a lunch of baguette ham sandwiches and hard-boiled eggs washed down with black coffee for the adults and water and soft drinks for the children. Before lunch, they swam in the river, the water fresh and warm from the sun warmed pebbles beneath. The sun dried them as they sat and ate.

But the wind had come up and this final phase back to the hire-base and their two cars, was requiring a more vigorous effort from them all. Head down and sweating cold in the wind, Thomas plunged the paddle in, trying to sustain a rhythm of strokes on either side of the canoe. He could feel his left hand blister but kept thrusting forward. Every-so-often the wind in the riverbank vegetation would catch his attention and he would glimpse the fluorescent silver and yellow petticoats of underleaf, flashing briefly in the wind. At intervals, he held his hand up into the draught of the wind. Once he plunged it into the water and then held it up for the wind to dry. An eagle wheeled high up above them.

He later watched eight griffin buzzards from the bridge at Les Millandes. He insisted on pulling the car over by the side of the road and indicated the birds to Judith and the children. He reached for the binoculars and, getting out of the car, glassed a distant ridge of holm-oak and chestnut trees.

This was an hour after returning the canoe to the hire centre, and the children were slumped exhausted in the car and he had difficulty holding and focussing as his shoulders and arms juddered slightly after the exertion on the river. The patronne of the hire centre, a feisty lady of hearty laugh, had mentioned the wind and how it had seemed to come from nowhere. Nevertheless, he got to watch the big birds whirl about on thermals over the ridge before they flew up into the sun and he was briefly blinded and when he could look again, they had dropped into the tree line and disappeared.

Two

NOT EVEN LAMBCHOP'S 'UP WITH PEOPLE' on the car's sound-system could rouse the children to singsong. Instead, they slept the way back to the campsite. Huge splats of rain smacked the windscreen, brought no doubt by the wind. More rain came later and put paid to their barbecue plans. They ate hachettes and frites at the site café. Thomas and Judith finished a Vin de Domme and went to bed.

It was a David and Goliath struggle in the dream that night with the reappearance of the man on board the Seacat, leaving Belfast. It was dark, yet Thomas had no trouble recognising the figure standing at the rail, his back to him. The piratical ponytail clicked metronomically, swung pendulously to and fro; it seemed to grow longer and bushier, the nearer Thomas drew. The man stood still and was unperturbed by the leucistic frenzy of water spewed out by the boat, inches away from him. Thomas put out his arms, palms forward, fingers pointing to the sky and increased his step. Then, at the last moment, as if endowed with some sixth sense, a built-in warning system, the man spun around and seized both of Thomas's extended hands and grinned in his face. Now they danced and grappled about the deck, bowling over unsuspecting on-loookers , by-standers and passers-by. All the time, his quarry seemed to grow and transmogrify in stature until he was towering above him and Thomas had to crane his neck back to see. By then, however, it had become a simple matter for him to hoist Thomas up off the deck and extend him out beyond the railing; from there he merely tossed Thomas off into the dark where, moments later, he found himself, awake, beside his wife, and bathed in sweat.

The next morning, Thomas sat on the terasse of the Café de Paris in Belvès. He ordered a grand crème and shook out the edition of Le Monde he had purchased in the newsagent's next door. The Tour had passed to the west of Belvès the previous day and Lance Armstrong, 'L'Homme de Fer', was maintaining pole position. The same wind that had chopped up the water on the river had blown into the faces of the riders and had slowed up that stage's progress.

He scanned the rest of the sports news and then turned, at last, to the inside of the paper, knowing he'd find there word of home. There would be unrest and tension and the ' marching season.' Belvès was a wonderful whorl of medieval dated houses and buildings, perched at a height; two steep roads led into it. The Café de Paris sat half-way down a narrow, pedestrianised thoroughfare and, at that time of the morning, the sun managed to flood the narrow space between the ornate, peeling buildings, and Thomas let a big, expansive breath out of him and looked up from the news report allowing the sun to warm his face. Yesterday's wind had blown itself out and the journal sat flat on the table. He sat with his eyes shut behind his sun-shades and, with the most recent dream still vivid in his head, made at last the effort to return his attention to the news report only for Patrice, who was just then passing, to speak suddenly to him.

— Les anges qui passent, laughed Patrice; and then gesturing to the chair at Thomas's table, said: Je vous dérange pas? Thomas was glad to see the man from Le Havre and assured him not at all.

The owner's son came from behind the counter and Patrice ordered a café and a glass of Vittel water. Patrice was one of the few French people that Thomas had managed to meet and converse with at any great length. The campsite, he had bemoaned, was mostly full of Dutch.

— Ah. Vous savez: Perigord, c'est la première departement hollandaise de La France, Patrice had quipped. It used to be the English, he went on. But they've mostly migrated further South.

The newspaper sat between them on the table-top and nodding at the opened headline Patrice asked him how things were at home. Thomas spoke of the spate of road blockades and illegal check-points and how shops and premises were mostly closing early; he attempted to explain about the marching season.

— Encore les Orangistes! Patrice interjected.

Thomas had to laugh then and Patrice reminded him that they were on holidays. Summoning the owner's son, he insisted on buying a drink. Thomas had a demi-pression; Patrice, a vin rouge. Thomas's glass came cold and beaded and the beer tasted good in the fine, forenoon sunshine.

— Lance is definitely going for his fifth then, Thomas said, turning the paper back to the sports pages. Though he seems to be doing it the hard way.

— A curious tour indeed, Patrice agreed.

Lance Armstrong had wiped out in a pile-up on the first stage. On the stage to Gap, he narrowly avoided careening into the Spaniard Joseba Beloki who had skidded on melted tar. He lost the first time trial to Jan Ullrich by 96 seconds because he was severely dehydrated. It was certainly a hot summer.

On his way back to the car, Thomas stopped off at the boulangerie; he bought bread for the lunch including a pain lardon, most of which he devoured himself, driving back to the camp-site. Driving down from Belvès, he lowered the window and gave the French countryside a blast of My Vitriol as he went.

That afternoon, they swam in the camp-site swimming pool and just as they were getting out and reaching for towels and cajoling the children to come too, lightning began to flick the summits of the mountains to the west of them. Judith reckoned the storm was far enough away to risk barbecuing. Thomas cooked mergère sausages and turkey-meat kebabs, swigging a couple of bottles of 33 as he did so; Judith prepared a garlic flavoured coucous and a salad. The air was deadly still and leaden and as it grew dark, even the bullfrogs went silent in the near-by lake. The children were both excited and nervous, but they were also exhausted by all the recent activities and they were soon asleep.

Thomas and Judith remained sitting outside, sipping their wine and sitting still and waiting for the storm to break. The air seemed tense and brittle around them and the distant thunder sounded high-pitched and dry, crackling more than rumbling. Then the still, steel-like leaves of the trees began to fidget nervously as the first vanguard of wind blew into the camp-site; a flurry of anxious foliage. They both took deep breaths, but the wind was hot and arid and they waited for the first drops of rain to fall and maybe cool things down. A great flash of phosphorescence petrified the campsite and moments later the thunder let out a deep-throated growl. This rumbled off and all was still again.

Once, in Kerry, on the Dingle Peninsula, they had made a mad drive to the beach in the rain and Thomas and Judith had whooped and roared and plunged into the churning sea; only: the children had sat on the beach, huddled together under an impromptu tent of beach towels and crying on account of the sharp, sandy wind and the breakers crashing loudly on the strand and Thomas and Judith had to come out promptly from the spilt milk white waves to console them. Soft drinks and crisps had to be bought in Paidi O'Sé's bar up the road, as a consequence.

Now, the children were in bed and Judith reached across and held Thomas's hand and leaned her head back and they both waited for the storm. However, everything seemed stuck and static and still and they were astounded to realise that the storm had obviously changed direction, almost at a right-angle and was now headed north, away from them. Lightning back-flashed the jagged mountain-tops away over to their right and the rain went off that way too.

— It's changed direction, Judith said and there was disappointment in her voice.

They sat and watched the storm recede and disappear.

— Come on, she eventually whispered. Enough of this. Time for bed.

Reluctantly, Thomas got up and followed her inside.

Three

— I BET YOU HE'S NOT EVEN from Dublin, Judith joked. It's a cover: he's probably in the CIA or something.

They had been invited to Andrew's and Carla's canvas-site for a meal. Andrew having mentioned how he had bumped into another couple from Belfast had prompted Thomas to tell about his Dubliner.

He had been kicking ball with Jason and Molly on the tarmac outside the mobile home and Jason had hit the ball hard and Thomas had to run to retrieve it. The tall, thin man stopped the ball and tapped it back to Thomas. He had a shock of white hair with a moustache to match. Thomas merci-ed the man even though he half-expected him to be Dutch; instead he was from Dublin and had wryly said:

— Isn't that great French for an Irishman!

— You just don't like him because he made fun of your French, Carla said.

— How'd he know you were from Ireland? Andrew asked.

— Our accents; or else he saw the IRL sticker on the car. In any case, he's one of those complaining types; says he's going to write to Eurosites to complain about the amount of Dutch there are.

— Correct me if I'm wrong; were you two not complaining about the self-same thing? Carla interrupted.

— Fine, fine. Thomas conceded the point.

Andrew emerged from the tent with a couple of beers.

— Why do you think he's in the CIA? Not that you two are paranoid are anything, he asked with a laugh.

— I was only joking, Judith defended herself.

— He did know an awful lot about the 'Nort', Thomas added.

— The 'Nort'? Andrew was puzzled.

— The North, Thomas translated. It's just a little unusual: him knowing places and even street-names. Like: Judith's from Bangor and he knew pubs and restaurants there.

— Let's not get carried away, Judith counselled. He obviously travels a lot, to and fro across the border.

— Doing what? Carla asked, intrigued. Did he say?

— He said something vague about setting up a charity; a Dublin-based charity that's trying to widen its span.

— In other words: he's a decent Christian man and you two are making fun of him.

— Well, Thomas had the last word. He shouldn't have made fun of my French.

Only it wasn't the last word. As they sat down outside to chicken cooked in an orange marinate, Thomas was reminded of the ostrich meat.

— Not him again, Carla said at the mention of the Dubliner. You're obsessed.

However Andrew was curious;

— Ostrich meat?

— Yes; apparently he deliberately drove to Lalinde because he saw some pamphlet or other advertising a farm that reared ducks and geese—

— And ostriches, Judith put in.

— He told me he bumped into a work-colleague, by sheer accident, in the supermarket. So he's cooking ostrich steaks for the colleague and his family tonight.

— Well I'm sorry we've nothing so grand on the menu, Andrew said.

— Let's leave the poor man alone, Judith said. Carla's right: you are obsessed with him.

With the children having eaten earlier, after the meal, Thomas and Andrew went looking for them. On their way, Andrew pointed out a car sitting adjacent to a tent and told Thomas that it belonged to the new Belfast couple.

— More than likely Protestant, Thomas proclaimed.

— Like myself and Carla, Andrew reminded him.

— And Judith too, as you know, Thomas said.

Andrew nevertheless shook his head, bemused by it all.

— Alright: how the hell can you tell? He enquired.

— The stickers.

Andrew re-examined the back of the car and began to catch on.

— The GB sticker instead of an IRL one?

— That and the NI sticker.

They walked on and Andrew continued to shake his head.

— Jesus, he said. What a way to live: always labelling each other; sizing one another up.

— I know. I know, Thomas conceded. Listen: it doesn't mean they're bad people.

Nevertheless, Andrew walked on without saying anything and after a while, Thomas added:

— Of course they do run the big risk of people thinking the sticker says NL!

By this stage, they were outside the bar area of the campsite.

— I need a drink, was Andrew's weary reply.

Four

THE HUGE PREHISTORIC MAMMOTH WAS PLASTIC and let out a pre-recorded roar , which convulsed the children in fits of giddy laughter. It was a moment of light relief in what had become a hot day, with the three children tired and fractious.

Their intention had been to visit Lascaux ll, the replica caves close to the originals. They had wound down into the Vezère valley to reach Montignac. At the tourist office there, Thomas managed to get a family ticket but for a visiting slot in two and a half hours' time.

Under a brightly striped awning, they sat at a sunwarmed, honey-toned café. The kids had ice-cream and Judith and Thomas drank Stella Artois beer. The ticket Thomas had purchased also gave entrance to the prehistoric theme park of Le Thot. They paid the café bill and headed in that direction, the children complaining about being cooped up again in the car and nor did they want to hear, this time, any more Yo La Tengo, on the stereo.

— My head's sore too, Judith said, siding with them.

Thomas reached and snapped the music off.

It was a hot day and the animals were subdued and in some cases hidden in sheds and shelters out of sight. The children turned their noses up at the cattle stench that seemed stuck to the hot air. Thomas eagerly pointed-out spike-maned Mongolian Przewalski horses but the children were tired and unimpressed. They did stop a moment to view a couple of lumbering, heavy— candlelabraed reindeer and the huge model mammoth brought that moment of brief relief but in the end they were glad to get back into the car.

— Turn the air-conditioning on, Judith pleaded.

Thomas did so and he also assured everyone that it would be a lot cooler in the Lascaux Caves. Laura let it be known that she didn't think it 'cool' at all, going to see a lot of paintings on walls.

— Just you wait till you see these ones, Thomas retorted. Judith sat beside him in the passenger seat and glanced doubtfully sideways at him but kept her own counsel; she knew how important this visit was to her husband.

They were not getting to see the original caves. Years of human intrusion, breathing moisture and bacteria onto the delicate filigrees and esquisses, colours and pigments, had begun to corrode and erase the cave paintings. Therefore, the French Government had poured a lot of time and money into funding the creation of replica grottes close to the original location. These were where they were going; and Thomas was excited, and the children's recalcitrance and his wife's circumspection, for he sensed, more than actually saw, her sideways look, could not dampen his expectations.

He had seen an earlier artificial version of the caves, some twenty years previously, in Le Grand Palais, in Paris; where he had been studying architecture. The artists had created a huge fibre-glass construction with subdued lighting and sound-proofing, to shut out the constant moan of city traffic. You cannot go back in time of course; but they had made a valiant effort at conjuring the illusion of stepping into a pre-historic series of coloured caves. They had even dropped the temperature by several degrees, the memory of which prompted him now to assure the others that it would be cold underground. All that had been so long ago; and Paris seemed like another country; but at long last he had made it to the Vezère Valley and he was excited. Even if he still wasn't getting to see the original paintings.

It was infectious, for by the time they pulled into the forest parking, the mood had changed in the car. Everyone was eager to get out and into the caves. It was cooler in the shade of the trees as they waited for the guide to lead them underground.

— When we get back, we'll have to go to Newgrange, he whispered to Judith as he watched the guide.

— When we get back, she replied, putting undue emphasis on the first word and then the crowd of tourists moved forward. Stick together, she shouted to the children.

Underground, all three children stared up and about and around them in awe, as did Judith and Thomas and the tourists, all huddled together in the narrow chambers and subterranean galleries. These beasts were not the paralysed, heat-dazed ones of Le Thot; rather they leapt out from their stillness across the cave walls in a motionless stampede of colour and composition.

The visitors bumped and stumbled through the cool, almost underwater half-light, illuminated at intervals with bursts of brightly coloured bison and blood-red deer and prehistoric stallions. On one surface, there was a string of horses with the lead one apparently only half-drawn; or else its bottom half had been eaten away. Something about this circumstance stopped Thomas and he stood and studied the composition.

— It is perspective, the French guide said to him in a hushed, almost reverential tone. She had come up and stood beside him.

— Mon Dieu, Thomas said, suddenly seeing it.

— You see? She said, pointing the horizontal line out with her finger floating in mid-air.

The horse was not poorly sketched nor half-drawn, not faded nor corroding; dating though the drawings did from the Upper Palaeolithic age, 18,000 years BC, nevertheless, these horses were receding into a distance, disappearing over some long-gone horizon.

The ancient artists knew about perspective.

— 'The days,' Thomas quoted, 'run away like wild horses over the hills.'

And there was room in this day for one further wonder as the girl responded:

— Ah. J'adore Bukowski.

Thomas turned around to get a better look at this girl but she had already moved on and was indistinct now in the ambient, subterranean gloom.

Five

— WELL. HOW WAS IT? JUDITH ASKED when they stood once more outside, above ground, under the pine-trees. The musk of the trees saturated the air about them. Was it as good as you expected?

The children were squealing and shouting and chasing each other around tree trunks. Thomas watched them a moment and then gave his verdict:

— Better, he confessed.

— Good, Judith said. Let's round the kids up and I'll drive and we'll stop off somewhere on the way back. You can have a few drinks to celebrate.

— Splendid idea, he suddenly boomed out, aping the refined, plumy accent of the retired army colonel and government official they had once met on a train from Budapest to Moscow.

In the car, they all sang along with 'Cherry Chapstick', making valiant, oral efforts to imitate the energetic bursts of feed-back and guitar.

As a reward for their perseverance, Thomas suggested they drive straight back to the campsite, no stop offs, and the children dashed off to the pool before it closed. Before cooking, Thomas and Judith sat on the terasse of the campsite bar. Thomas manoeuvred his seat out from under the shade of the parasol and sat in the late evening sun. Some of the campsite workers were setting up a big movie screen for that night's outdoor cinema presentation under the stars. The thought of moving images being thrown up against the gable end of the main estate building brought back the day's earlier images and Thomas expressed again his pleasure at having seen the caves.

— Though it's still a pity you can't actually see the real thing, Judith said.

— God you sound like Jean Baudrillard, Thomas declared. In 'The Precession of Simulacra', Baudrillard had mentioned Lascaux, saying: 'The duplication of the caves rendered both artificial'.

— The false has taken over the original, Judith continued and then hastened to say: Though you still enjoyed the visit; didn't you.

— Listen. Don't let's forget that for me the 'original' Lascaux caves were those fibre glass ones I saw twenty years ago in Paris. Somehow, I think Baudrillard would approve.

And somehow Jean Baudrillard brought him back to his hometown. It was the occasion, just three months before coming to France, of the funeral of a former classmate.

He had watched while officials for the fighters and the football club debated outside the wake house. In the end the party prevailed and only the flag bedecked the coffin while the club jersey was held in prominent view as the cortege began the long march to the graveyard.

As he fell in behind the procession, he lost count of the number of lifts the coffin got. People queued to carry the comrade and/or team-mate. A massive crowd lined the streets as the long cortege wound its way down the hill and across the town. As they inched along he got an increasing impression that something was not as it should be. Distracted by the fact that at intervals, along the way, he had to nod to or shake hands with people he had not seen for years, he tried to concentrate on what it was that was nagging at him. Passing side streets and entries he peered down them and saw nothing. He scanned the tops of buildings on the route; over his shoulders there were only mourners.

The graveyard on the opposite hillside was full of living people and at a distance from the grave, he could just about make out the speeches and orations. In a neighbouring field a horse box rattled up to a gate; the driver waited while a young girl got out to open it. The horse's whinny carried across to the graveyard as it clattered down the ramp. At first uncertain about its release from the box, it hesitated and flexed its long neck and snorted the air. Then, with a sudden surge of energy, it was off, up the slope of the field and as Thomas's eye followed it to the skyline and as he realised he could hear the hollow thud of its hooves on the turf, only then did he comprehend his intuition; and the hairs stood up on the back of his neck.

Astounded he surveyed all around him just to be sure: the crowded town was empty.

His image was not caught in any cross-hairs; there were no hi-tech surveillance cameras, no high-definition lenses, no binoculars, observers, check-points, concealed convoys of waiting land-rovers, police cars; no caterwaul of rotor blades drowning out orations and prayers, no downdraughts scattering hats and headscarves - handkerchiefs; no unmarked cars, spies-in-the-sky; ranks of riot shields leaning Trojan-like in side streets ready to be snatched up; no rubber bullets, batons nor tear-gas; no 'PIGs' nor water cannons, nor dragon teeth; no Saracens; no metallic, megaphone voice booming from on high.

No riot.

Mourners merely walked back down into the town. Thomas went down in the company of two he had played club football with and they stopped for a pint in 'The Brass Monkey'.

— I suppose you can hardly recognise the place, one of them said.

— Big changes, the other added.

They meant the shopping centres and the rash of housing projects up onto and over the shoulders of the low mountains encircling the town and the fact that the town was now a city. Thomas shared with them what he meant by change, what he had just that afternoon realised. However, they shook their heads as they listened to him.

— They're still here, one of them said.

— What?

— They're in the air, the other explained. Mobile phones? E-mails? Computers? The internet.

— I guarantee you someone was watching, they had both assured him.

As if to illustrate their point an 'Amhran na bhFiann' ring tone rang out prompting a man in overalls sitting at the bar to produce his mobile phone and proceed to shout into it.

— Soon everyone will have a mobile phone and then they'll have no problem keeping tabs on you.

This is how he found himself sitting in The Brass Monkey bar thinking of Jean Baudrillard.

Six

THE HOTEL, LOCATED IN PLACE DE la Croix-des-Frères in Belvès, is called Le Home.

Two days after Lascaux, Thomas and Judith sat on the terasse of the café opposite, having a drink before going for dinner in the hotel. They had booked a table earlier on in the day, once Andrew and Carla had said they would mind the children for the night. However, it was Saturday evening and awfully quiet in the little town.

— It's early yet, Thomas said. Surely things have got to liven up.

A waiter, in a white apron, was leaning in the door-way behind them.

— Maybe we should have driven into Bergerac, Judith said, reaching for her panaché. It's not that far.

— We're here now, Thomas declared.

A mother and father, with a grown-up son and daughter and a younger daughter of around thirteen or fourteen, appeared into the square and crossed over to the hotel. They watched this family crowd round the glass display-cabinet that housed the daily menus. The mother detached herself from the group and disappeared inside only to emerge minutes later and usher the family on up the street.

Judith and Thomas exchanged glances.

— Or Sarlat, Judith suggested.

— Stop it. Thomas said. We're staying put. He turned and roused the waiter from his stupor and ordered another beer for himself. This time, Judith went for a kir royal.

A Saab pulled into a parking space directly opposite them and after a few minutes, in which the occupants seemed to be deliberating, a middle-aged man and a woman some years his junior got out. They glanced over at the café and then the man spotted Le Home and they went there and went inside without looking at the menus.

— C'est un peu tranquille, Thomas suggested to the waiter as he returned with their drinks.

— N'est-ce pas! Was all he returned and he went and resumed his place in the door-way.

The church clock took its time chiming out the hour.

— The children away, we should be thankful for a bit of peace and quiet.

— A wee bit of excitement wouldn't go amiss though, Judith said.

— Later, babe, later, Thomas vowed.

— I said excitement, Judith replied.

Two locals came down the hill and swinging their hips through the maze of out-door tables, greeted the waiter and all three disappeared indoors. Soon, the juke-box came to life and belted out a Johnny Halliday song , which stirred up the air a bit. A woman came to a window opposite and looked out.

— You never know: this could well be the place to be, later on, Thomas surmised.

— Whatever, Judith said. Let's go and eat. I'm starving.

They were pleasantly taken aback by how noisy the hotel was, the nearer they got to it. The dining room was full except for their reserved table over by the window. The clientele looked mostly local, with the man and girl, from the Saab, seated at a table in the centre of the high-ceilinged, rustic room.

They ordered the local, house red before considering the hand-printed menus, given to them by a plump, pleasant waitress. From the window, they spied more locals, some pulling up on mopeds, going into the café. Judith reached across the white, linen tablecloth and squeezed his hand.

— This is nice, isn't it, she said.

They started with a basil and tomato soup, served out of a huge, vaporous tureen. This they drank up eagerly, breaking off chunks of coarse-grained country bread with which to wipe their bowls clean. On request, the waitress came and milled thick black pepper on Thomas's soup.

Eventually, Thomas sighed and sat back. He took in, then, the surroundings and wondered aloud if they shouldn't perhaps have had booked a room for the night.

— Sure we have the mobile to ourselves, tonight, Judith said. And hopefully we'll get a sleep-in the morning.

However, as Judith was saying this, Thomas was looking at two gendarmes tiptoeing out through the swing-doors from the kitchen. Two more flashed past the window to his right. A barely perceptible lull or suspension seemed to settle on the dining-room and perhaps it was this that alerted the man from the Saab; for his back was to the kitchen. Or perhaps he read something in his companion's facial expression. In any case, his reflexes were amazing for he was almost to his feet before the two policemen were on top of him. There was instant uproar and the neighbouring table overturned. The man was baying like some wild animal, as he was strangled and grappled to the floor and handcuffed and restrained.

The dining room milled with gendarmes now and the screaming girl was spirited away. The Saab man was lifted bodily and borne off out the door and with him went all sense of movement. Diners and waitresses remained frozen to the spot. This was broken then by the appearance of a senior police official whose French Thomas had difficulty following as he attempted to give assurances to everyone who had witnessed the incident. He gave the vaguest of explanations and urged them all to resume their meals. The family whose table had been overturned, he invited outside for a brief interview.

Only then was there a sudden release of pent-up debate and speculation: people gesticulating and waving their arms about and Thomas realised that all this time he had had a grip of Judith's arm, having reached for it across the table. He gave it a comforting pat now and as she continued to peer all around her and out the window, he quietly replaced the steak-knife beside his plate, from where he had deftly snatched it up, moments before.

Seven

HIS FATHER WAS IN A KNIFE-fight once, during The Second World War, with an on-leave, American GI. It happened in that busy market town his father, and later he, grew up in, located close to the border.

His father owned a public house on the main street a few doors down from The Frontier Cinema. American troops would have been stationed in camp-sites scattered around the countryside and, often at weekends, the soldiers would flood into the town on leave. However, the knife-fight took place early one week-day. His father had just opened the doors with the Spike Davis (something to do with his having worked once on the railways in Canada) the sole client requiring admission at such an early hour; he quickly ensconced himself, out of the way, in the snug at the main street side of the bar — there was an entrance in off the side street as well — and subsequently missed the whole action, oblivious to the two large men crashing into furniture, counter and walls. The snug, it should be said, was meant really for female clientele where they could sup in peace, nodding their chins and ordering sherry and gin through the confessional of the hatch door that opened onto the counter at that end. The Spike Davis favoured the snug at that early, normally empty hour.

At that time, his father washed the empties and bottled, capped and labelled the beer himself. Arthur Guinness supplied him with customised labels for the bottles. These stickers included the name of the proprietor, deftly printed in around that distinctive company design. Having let the Spike Davis in and served him his bottle of stout and measure of rum, his father had disappeared out the back to retrieve a newly bottled crate of beer from the bottling store. The way back in led past the stairway winding up to the living quarters. Glancing up, he suddenly stopped in his tracks at the sight of the uniformed American half-way up the stairs. At this point, his teenaged younger sister, just in from morning mass, must also have seen the GI for she let out a scream from above, out of sight, just around the turn of the landing. The soldier had obviously followed her home and in through the side door, stalking her on up the stairs.

His father let the crate drop, took the stairs, two at a time, yanked the soldier by the shoulder and pitched him down the stairs into the back hall, swimming now with beer. The soldier was quickly to his feet, though he had trouble steadying himself what with slipping in the spillage and then barking his shin on the discarded, wooden beer-crate. In such stumbling fashion, he disappeared into the bar area. Thomas's father leapt down after him.

Turning the corner, he found himself confronted with the GI, seething, crouched over with a flick knife open in his right hand. He immediately regretted not lifting a bottle from the crate for protection; he even fleetingly thought of fashioning a vambrace from his long, white, vintner's apron.

— His arm, Thomas's father would say, the few occasions he could be cajoled into recounting the event. I quickly realised that I had to get a grip of his right arm and just hold on for day life.

Possibly still dazed from the tumble over the crate of beer, the soldier did not anticipate his assailant's swift move. His father got a vice-like grip of the right arm and, linked like this, the two men waltzed on into the bar cursing and struggling and strangling and whirling each other around.

What saved his father was the ancient and imposing structure of the dark brown mahogany counter that ran the length of the bar. At one point, the two combatants came careening off the back wall and they collided with the counter. The tip of the blade of the flick-knife struck the unyielding, obsidian surface of the wood and bounced right back off it. The soldier must not have had a firm grasp of the handle for, at the shock of impact, the blade slid up his grip, slicing open the palm of his hand, incising on up over his wrist. The knife clattered to the flag-stone floor and, extricating himself, the GI exited the bar, baying, his father always said, like some wounded beast. As he went, spraying blood about him, the Spike Davis chose that moment to slide open the hatch and, spying Thomas's father standing panting where he was, requested another rum and stout.

— The knife, dad, Thomas's older brother had once asked. What did you do with the knife?

They were both hoping that it existed as some sort of grisly, family heirloom.

— I gave it to Joseph Slow Waters; as evidence.

Their father had become friendly with a military policeman. Joseph Slow Waters was of the Navaho nation and although he did not take alcohol he liked to visit the bar, when on leave, and stand at the counter and chat quietly to their father, at slack times, and to any of the locals who cared to listen and respond.

Joseph Slow Waters was enraged when his father reported the incident and, taking the knife away, vowed to be on the look-out for a GI with heavily bandaged hand and wrist.

— And God help him if he was ever caught, their father would say. Those Military Police boys took no prisoners!

Thomas's father never discovered if the culprit was caught. Almost overnight, the camps emptied and the soldiers disappeared; they found themselves on board a fleet of warships, forging their way across a porter-dark sea, bound for the beaches of Normandy.

A soldier with a heavily bandaged hand and wrist would quickly find familiars there.

There were soldiers too in the town, when Thomas was growing up. These ones, as you know, were not on leave.

Eight

— YOU'VE FOUND THE COOKER THEN, THE Dubliner said, standing outside on the steps of the mobile-home, but craning his neck inside.

— Ha, ha, Thomas said.

He was scrubbing the hob-top clean as part of the preparation for leaving the camp-site, the next day.

— What about the hoover, the Dubliner persevered with his conceit. Have you found out where that's kept yet?

A second time, Thomas gave a half-laugh, but he still told Nial to come in; at least he hadn't just barged on in uninvited. Furthermore, he had left-over groceries to give them.

— We're heading off home today. Thought you could use these. Shame them going to waste.

Judith was out dumping rubbish, as they spoke. There was a

sturdy, wooden stockade, at the entrance to the camp and she and the children had driven down there with a load of bound up bin-liners, and a cardboard box of empties.

— That's very kind of you, Thomas assured Nial. No: it'll not go to waste. The kettle's just boiled -

— That's okay, Nial declined. Got to get back to the packing.

Despite this, he sat down , jack-knifing his lanky legs in under the dining table. Thomas put down the scrubbing pad he had been using and wiped his greasy hands on some kitchen-roll.

— What time do you hope to get away for? He enquired, feigning interest.

— I'm aiming to be on the road in about an hour. But tell me, Nial went on. That was a bit of excitement up in the town the other night.

— You heard about it? Thomas asked.

— Sure weren't we there? We saw the whole hullabaloo.

— You were up in Belvès? Thomas said.

— Remember I told you about that work colleague I bumped into? We were supposed to go to his site for a barbecue only they decided suddenly, out of the blue, to drive down to Toulouse and take a flight up to Eurodisney. So we were left having to go into Belvès, to look for something to eat. It was very inconvenient; but what can you do?

— Ostrich steaks all gone? Thomas asked.

— Devoured. Days ago, Nial assured him. Anyway: we saw the police throwing your man into the back of a van and then we spotted you two through the window. You looked very unflustered by it all.

The Hotel had given everyone a complimentary liqueur and Thomas and Judith had had a few more drinks and, with the mobile to themselves, they had had a fine time of it, later on. The local paper, on the Monday, reported that a serial rapist had been apprehended in Belvès on the previous Saturday night. It somehow besmirched the fun they had had.

— A serial rapist? Nial mused, this being news to him.

44

— Apparently, he was being tracked from Biarritz. According to the paper. Thomas said.

— God. And that young girl was to be his next victim; more than likely, Nial theorised.

There was a pause while they both contemplated this.

— Either that or she was undercover, Nial then went on. This hadn't occurred to Thomas.

— One way or another, Thomas said. She was damned lucky.

— Good old gendarmes, Nial said, getting to his feet.

— Listen, Thomas stated. Thanks again for these. He indicated the two plastic bags.

They shook hands and wished each other a safe journey home.

— When are you heading home yourself? Nial enquired, standing once more outside the mobile.

— Oh, we've a few weeks yet, Thomas answered vaguely.

— Well you never know: I might bump into you all up North. Maybe in Bangor. And with that, he walked off, turning once to wave.

Thomas went back inside and unpacked the plastic bags. There were five cans of Heinekin; three eggs, a jar of mayonnaise, some long-life milk, a jar of peanut butter, instant coffee, coffee filters and some Nesquit chocolate cereal.

— That was nice of him, Judith observed, when she came in and he explained the items sitting on the work surface beside the sink.

— Beware the Greeks when they bear you gifts, Thomas warned unkindly.

— You ungrateful pig, she called him.

— Who is? Laura asked climbing up the steps and only having half-heard.

— Your father, Judith answered.

— Oh, come on, Thomas insisted. I was only joking.

— What's this? Jason asked, holding up the jar of peanut butter.

45

— I don't think it's your cup of tea, Thomas advised. Try it and see.

They made use of all the items except the peanut butter; it didn't make it.

Nine

THOMAS WAS SURPRISED WHEN HE REALISED how often, here in France, they found themselves surrounded by Protestants.

It struck him first in the Bastide Country as he stood marvelling at the arcaded and cloistered, main square of Monpazier. The sun beat down on the yellowed, fine old buildings and Thomas observed:

— You almost expect Michael York and Oliver Reed to come swaggering around the corner.

— Hardly! Judith corrected.

— No, I mean it. It looks like a film set.

— I know what you mean; but they were musketeers, she explained. They were on Richelieu's side.

— But Richelieu was their enemy.

— Yes, but they were on the same side. This was a Protestant fortified town.

— Alright. I see what you mean, Thomas conceded.

They had briefly lost sight of the children who had been lured into the shaded walkways by the bright array of trinkets and bracelets and necklaces, bewebbing the whirly-display stands located there. Then Laura appeared at one of the corners of the Square, calling to them and waving them over. They hastened across the sun-drenched clearing and plunged into the shade, taking a moment for their eyes to adjust.

— You've got to take a photograph, she was urging them. Look.

It was a French street name that amused her so: Rue Pont d'Ormeau.

— Well spotted, Thomas congratulated his eldest daughter. You're right: we've got to get a picture. You two stand under it.

The sign was fixed to the wall of a Seventeenth Century building and in the view-finder he could also get in one of the arcades funnelling off down the west side of the Square as if one of the arches was endlessly repeating itself off into the distance.

Thomas had bought the IRL sticker for the car in his local version of the Ormeau Road.

The car-parts and accessory shop was just before the Bridge which demarcated where the Upper Ormeau ended and the Lower one began; the Lower was a Nationalist area. The little grid of back-streets, surrounding the car shop, was not. In the run-up to the marching season, these streets and house-fronts fluttered like a Kurosawa movie; albeit with Union Jacks and St. George's Crosses. So Thomas entered the shop on the half-chance; not expecting to find the sticker of his choice.

A youth in his twenties with a number one haircut and wearing a blue shop-coat looked up at him from behind the counter. Thomas tried to size him up without making eye-contact. He pretended to browse among cans of spray-paint and wind-screen wipers.

— You've got to read this, Judith urged, tapping the visitors' brochure about Monpazier.

Things had not been easy in that area in the Seventeenth Century. The religious war brought bitter hardship, and, as a result, there had been a series of peasant uprisings against the misery caused by the wars. However, Judith was drawing his attention to the slightly more light-hearted account by the Protestant general Sully of how the men in the Catholic bastide of Villefranche de Périgord stole through the night to capture Monpazier. They found the town mystifyingly easy to ransack. This was because, as coincidence would have it, the men of Montpazier were off, the very same night, but by a different route, pillaging Villefranche de Perigord. Meeting no resistance, both sides looted to their hearts' content. The subsequent peace terms were that everyone should return everything to its proper place.

— It's typically Irish, Thomas quipped.

— Can I help you? The youth in the accessory shop asked him.

— Turtle-wax, Thomas hastily replied. And stickers. You know: for the car, going on holidays.

The youth pointed to a whirly-stand of stickers which only now Thomas noticed and his heart sank when all he could spot were GBs and NIs. Then, low down and dusty, he saw the IRL stickers; he took two with him up to the counter.

— Actually, I don't need the Turtle-wax, he said to the youth. Just these.

— No problem, the youth assured him, replacing the bottle on the shelf behind him.

— Ce n'est pas un problème, the girl behind the counter in the visitors' centre in the Tour de la Chaine, in La Rochelle, assured him. He was apologising for having to pay for two plastic models of musketeers, on horse-back, with a fifty euro note.

— Come on: own up, Judith ribbed him. You didn't buy them for Jason at all. You bought them for yourself.

— You've got to admit: they are cool, he replied, holding them up admiringly.

— Have you ever told the children about your famous swordsmanship? She mischievously enquired.

— Very amusing, he replied.

He also bought a postcard reproduction of 'Siège de 1628, Richelieu sur la digue,' by Henri Motte. Standing apart from a huddled group of mostly clerics, Richelieu has his arms folded across his armoured breast-plate and his hawk-like profile is coldly surveying the starving town, encircled as it is by his man-made, wooden dykes. He is unperturbed as, inches from his knee-length riding-boots, the sea churns up and his cardinal's cape blows out behind him in the wind.

Ten

BEER IS A TIME MACHINE.

Having invited Andrew, Carla and kids for a final meal, Thomas had had a few beers at the mobile home and was now ordering four more at the campsite, poolside bar.

— None for me, Andrew said. Not with the long drive home tomorrow.

— Trois bières, alors, Thomas ordered.

— Three beers? The Dutch waitress said.

— Oui. Trois bières.

— Really though, Judith was saying to Carla and Andrew. You must come over and visit us. It's perfectly safe.

— It must have been difficult for you two, in the old days, being a mixed marriage?

— Andrew!

— No. That's alright. We had a few problems at first. From family. Didn't we?

— A few; but love prevailed!

— What about between yourselves. Does it ever cause any rows?

— God. Yes. Thomas is always wallowing in his victimhood.

— I am not. Anyway, I've more to be a victim about than you: growing up in your nice, cosy seaside resort.

— I hope I haven't started something.

— Oh, come on now, Judith insisted. Your lot love all that suffering. When were you ever really a victim?

Thomas sat forward in his seat and regarded Carla and Andrew.

— The Devil, he announced to Carla and Andrew. Came to my hometown in nineteen seventy five. It was the same year that Bernadette Devlin came to a rally at the top of our street.

— They don't know who Bernadette Devlin is.

— I think I've heard of her.

— She was a leading figure back then in the Civil Rights Movement. I remember there was a big crowd gathered and John Bull's flying machine was hovering overhead and my older brother and I pushed our way to the front. She was wearing a miniskirt and dufflecoat and was hoisted up on people's shoulders but my brother still managed to get her autograph on a copy of An Phoblacht.

— They don't know what that is either.

— Does your brother still have the autograph?

— No. Days later, we heard that the army was doing house-to-house searches and my dad went upstairs and scooped up my brother's political books and wrapping them in that issue of An Phoblacht pitched the whole bundle over the wall into the coal-yards behind our house.

— And: the Devil?

— Well; devil worshippers to be precise. People's pets had started going missing. Then mutilated carcasses began to turn up around the town, on a piece of waste ground at one end, dangling from the branches of trees in woodland at the other. Ritualistic sacrifices, word had it. More animals disappeared; cats, dogs. A donkey, if memory serves me right. It seemed like it would only be a matter of time before a child was snatched and panic gripped the town. S'il vous plaît? Encore trois.

— Not for me. I 've enough here.

— Deux. Schools warned parents and pupils. I remember we had this great teacher who took us that year for RE. We loved his classes because he didn't actually teach RE. Instead we had discussions. About anything under the sun. Well, he warned us that if we were going home after football practice that we were to keep in twos and threes. Not to be walking on our own. Of course, we all thought we were hard men, back then, but he quickly assured us that if they wanted to snatch us they'd be able to bundle us into a car no bother. ' Don't think you'll be able to kick them in the balls and run', he said to us. Well that really freaked us out. And then, to top it all off, our parents would hardly let us out in the evenings. Merci.

— This is my round, Andrew insisted.

— Anyway, this state of affairs lasted for a month or two. Then, one day, it was all over. I remember Gerry Cahill coming into school and assuring us that he had heard that the 'boys' had caught up with the perpetrators and had 'sorted them out', so to speak. Things gradually got back to normal, and we were allowed back out on the streets.

— I can't see what this has got to do with you being a victim.

— That's because I'm not finished yet.

— Well I wish you'd hurry up. I'm sure Carla and Andrew would like to get back to Scotland this summer.

— Okay. Fast forward to only a couple of years ago. There was a book published by an ex-colonel in the S.A.S. In it, he describes the various dirty tricks campaigns the army waged in the North and one of them, it seems, entailed spreading rumours of devil worship in a small town near the border. My fucking town. He boasted how successful it had been in keeping the local youths, who would otherwise have been out throwing stones and bottles at the soldiers, off the streets for a couple of weeks. They had made the whole thing up; all that time they had been messing with my fucking mind. All that time to have believed that we had been in danger of being kidnapped and cut up. And only to have learned the truth just a couple of years ago.

Thomas lifted his bottle off the table and sat back again in his seat.

After the exchanges of hugs and kisses and addresses and the shakings of hands, Carla and Andrew departed and Judith and Thomas made their way back to the mobile home. The night air was stern with the sound of zips and Judith told Thomas to keep his voice down as he spoke.

— Do you want to know what I really remember about seeing Bernadette Devlin that time? he said in a half-whisper.

— No.

— When they hoisted her up on their shoulders, it was the first time I ever saw up a grown woman's skirt.

— You're disgusting.

— I know, he assured his wife as they arrived at their van. I'm going to sit outside for a while.

— What about my skirt? She enquired.

— You're not wearing a skirt.

— I was speaking metaphorically; but forget it. The moment's past.

Thomas sat outside for a long time. He was sitting in the middle of France, under the trees of the little woodland among which the site's mobile homes were situated. It was warm enough to sit outside in just the zip-up cardigan he wore. There was the sough of a breeze in the foliage above his head and he heard the soft percussive bursts of ripe cherries on the roof of the car. Suddenly weary, he found himself wondering about all the cyclists lying dormant out there in the dark French paysage.

—How do they keep going? he mused aloud.

His laughter a moment later brought his wife to the van door.

— Would you come to bed, Thomas. Do you know what time it is?

— Yes I do, he declared.

He roused himself in his seat and, looking at his wife, said:

— Time for a beer, ma cherie.

Eleven

A 'YOLE' IS A LOCAL, VENDÉEN, flat-bottomed boat, specifically adapted to the salt marshes of the area and the maraîchins still use it today for pleasure and business, both commercial and religious. La Yole was also the name of the new campsite they were trying to find.

They had underestimated the length of the drive to the west coast from the Dordogne and it was late afternoon by the time they drove into St Jean de Monts. They cruised slowly along the stretch of road that ran parallel to the beach, La Plage des Mouettes. Although tired and with eyes peeled for sign-posts for the campsite, the name of the beach registered with Thomas and he realised that for three weeks he had been out of ear-shot of these particular birds.

— Eagles? Jason misheard.

— Seagulls! Judith corrected and although she was driving she still patted her husband on the knee and said with mock-concern, The long drive getting to you darling?

The children joined in:

— Yes, dad, they chorused. Did you miss your sea-gulls?

— It just made me realise that, for you brats, the Dorgogne is the farthest in-land you've ever been. That's all. He sternly explained. Now. Keep looking for sign-posts.

The girl at reception welcomed Thomas's use of French. For Thomas, it was amusing being able, at last, to put a face to the voice of the person with whom he had booked the mobile-home the previous month. She got their details up on screen and took key and bed-linen deposits from him. Then she marched him outside to demonstrate the lifting and lowering of the electronic barrier giving access to the camp.

— You are parked where? She enquired of Thomas.

Judith had pulled into a small parking area on the side of the road opposite the camp entrance. The girl requested that the car be brought up to the barrier in order for her to do her demonstration. Thomas waved Judith to come over. Judith cocked her eyebrows at Thomas and the children stared wide-eyed at the girl's sudden, officious, brash manner. The special plastic card-key was of particular concern to her. Gravely, she showed them the right side up for inserting the card and she even leaned in through the driver's window, reaching across Judith, and slapping the card down on the dashboard.

— This, she warned. You must not do.

— Le soleil, Thomas said to show he understood.

— C'est ça. It can cause damage to the card, she explained. Now: you will open the barrier and I will get my bicycle and you will follow me.

— Phew, said Laura, once they were through the barrier. I'm glad we passed that test.

The girl became pleasant once more on ushering them into the mobile home and seeing how impressed they were by the bright, spacious interior. She seemed to take a personal pride in the caravan and she stood and watched the family explore the various nooks and crannies and smiled and nodded when they uttered anything approving, in French or English.

Once the girl had gone off, wishing them a pleasant stay, they unpacked enough to realise just how tired they were after the drive. Exhaustion clung to them like a clammy, second skin; so they abandoned the unpacking and all went off to find the bar-café area. They spotted an outdoor table in the sun, overlooking the pool complex. The children raided the ice-lolly freezer and Judith and Thomas ordered beers and collapsed into their seats. They deliberately avoided sizing up the pool area and the camp-site, knowing as they did how unreliable first impressions of a place can be, especially if you are tired after a long, arduous journey. They sat and said nothing and only roused themselves to lift their glasses and quaff some beer. Gradually, the children returned and they too were tired and according to them the campsite was not anywhere as good as the one they had left in the Dorgogne.

— Wait till you see it tomorrow, Thomas counselled them. We're all tired; we'll get something to eat and then have an early night.

Spying a waiter carrying what looked like menus, he caught his attention and called him over, saying:

— S'il vous plâit?

The young man cheerfully took their order.

The next day, a warm sea breeze blew, and, after the storms and thunder in the Dorgodne, everyone had suddenly sprouted sun-shades.

Twelve

WITH BREAD FROM THE CAMPSITE SHOP and ham and cheese transported in the cool bag from the Dordogne, they breakfasted well and prepared a simple picnic of coffee, juice, water and fruit. Before leaving the mobile, they smeared themselves with sun-cream. They packed beach-bags with swimwear and goggles, brought football and tennis rackets and books and buckets and spades and headed for the beach at Les Sables d'Olonne.

The beach stretched for miles and the town itself curved concentrically around the sea front with high-rise flats and offices overlooking the thousands of sun-seekers. Office workers and shop assistants appeared at lunch-time and stripped down to swim-wear and many of the girls went topless and lay in the sun. Most would reappear at the end of the working day. At intervals, as he read the previous day's newspaper, Thomas would cast discreet glances to right and left.

He wanted to catch up with Lance Armstrong. The stage to Luz-Ardiden had been yet another incident filled ordeal. Armstrong had started the day just 15 seconds ahead of Jan Ullrich. During the stage, he crashed, caught up, nearly crashed again, and then blasted past everyone to carry the day. At the press conference afterwards, he said:

' ... this has been the Tour of too many problems. Too many close calls, too many near misses ... I wish I could just have some uneventful days ... '

Thomas then dozed for a while, his head pillowed softly against Judith's thigh. She sat back against the base of the precipitous promenade wall and read Service's biography of Lenin. Jason, Molly and Laura dug in the sand and played there for some time before, finally, throwing the buckets and spades up to Judith and Thomas, for them to mind, and dashing down the beach to splash and swim in the sea. Judith watched them so that she knew where to locate them in the crowded surf; then, as she went to resume her reading, Thomas started suddenly in his doze and woke up.

— Guilty conscience? Judith suggested.

— Bad dream. Where are the kids?

Thomas sat up and after watching the children for a few moments he rummaged in the side pocket of the red beach-bag and fished out his goggles.

— I'm away to join them, he said.

— I'll stay and keep an eye on our stuff. Come up in a wee while and let me in, Judith called after him as he jogged off down the beach.

In such a way they came and went into the water and everyone got the chance to swim. Later, the tide went out and exposed a large swathe of hard, compact sand, the surface of which took a tennis ball and Jason and Molly played sand singles and Thomas kicked football with Laura. Her prowess drew admiring glances from some of the beach people sitting sunning themselves just up from where they played.

They stayed on the beach until early evening. The fresh sea breeze and the sun, the swimming and ball games made them all deliciously tired; not the cobwebby tiredness of the previous day. When they eventually left the beach, they were all disinclined to climb back into the car. They off-loaded the beach baggage and strolled leisurely along the promenade. Then, taking care with the seafront traffic, they crossed the road away from the seaside and entered the labyrinth of tiny back streets.

It was here he thought he saw him.

Thirteen

IT WAS THE MAN EYE-BALLING him that first alerted Thomas.

In the maze of back streets and alleys of the Old Quarter, away from the breeze of the beach, the heat had suddenly increased. The Quarter had, in recent years, received a tourist make-over, with which came a proliferation of ceramics shops and art galleries; there were designer boutiques and specialist patisseries and artisanal confectioneries. Most of the area was pedestrianised and, at that time of the evening, hiving with people. Thomas and Judith and the kids wandered for a while, stopping occasionally in the welcome cool of a shop awning. Jason was especially concerned about any one of their number going astray in the bustling back streets. He gripped his father's hand and kept a running commentary up as regards his older, more adventurous sisters' whereabouts. Often, the sisters would lag behind, entranced by jewellery displays, shaking up sand scenes of Les Sables d'Olonne, holding conch shells to their ears; and Jason would pull on Thomas's hand to stall him and so not lose sight of the girls.

— Come on girls, Thomas would shout back at them.

Where's mum? would be Jason's next concern, the minute he was satisfied the girls were once more back in step; some craft shop or boutique would have accounted for her disappearance.

— There she is, Molly would shout out and promptly disappear off in that direction with Jason bobbing like a boxer to keep sight of her through the bodies milling about him.

They eventually emerged into a little square and Thomas ushered them all onto the terrasse of a small sun-side café. He ordered a beer for himself, a glass of muscadet for Judith and Oranginas for the children; then he settled back for a breather. Tourists and locals went to and fro past their table. They were well away now from the beach but he could smell the sea-salt on the air. He sighed and reached for his beer and took a long, cold draught of it while Molly and Jason quickly drained their own drinks and began rattling the ice-cubes that remained in an effort to make them melt more quickly.

The man was sitting at a table in the interior of the café towards the back and Thomas at first did not see him as his eyes had to adjust from the glare outside. The toilets were in the basement and Thomas's eyes met the man's when he climbed back up the stairs and was briefly at eye-level with him. He stared Thomas out without the slightest nod or movement and Thomas returned to the terrasse a little bemused. It was only on the way back to the car that the resemblance struck Thomas and he stopped dead in his tracks. The abrupt stop jerked Jason back by the hand and he stared and was prompted to enquire:

— What's the matter, Dad?

— Nothing, Thomas replied but he tightened his grip on

Jason's hand and ordering the girls away from a postcard display, he herded them all back to the shore front. By the time he got to the car he was convinced that the man in the cafe was the spitting image of the Saab man from Belvès.

Claiming a sudden need to visit, after all, a bookshop he had walked past earlier, he left Judith and the children complaining loudly, and, hastened back in the direction of the café. He jogged and jostled his way through the strolling crowds of tourists and window-shoppers, bringing down curses upon himself from individuals he accidentally bumped into or brushed roughly past. He was soaked in sweat by the time he burst into the little square. He hung back a moment, contemplating the café front, straining to see into its dark depths from outside. He needed to know that he had been mistaken. He thought of the mad-eyed man he had met on the voyage out and this spurred him into action. He went up to and into the café. Two elderly men were putting out chess pieces at the table in question. They looked up at him as he entered. He nodded and went and looked down the stair well to the basement. He listened but there was too much noise from the square to allow him to judge whether there was anyone downstairs. So, he held his breath and began his descent. No matter how he positioned his feet or distributed his weight, the wooden stair treads groaned and complained beneath him. Half-way down he regretted not lifting a beer bottle from one of the tables on the way past. Empty-handed he approached the door to the sole toilet down there and with his foot edged it open. He let out a shout and half raised his hand and felt instantly embarrassed as a woman spun around on him suddenly from the mirror and challenged him for sneaking up behind her. Apologising, he made two bumbling attempts to close back over the door and stumbled back up the stairs and quickly left the café as he could hear her imprecations rising up behind him and one of the old men get growling to his feet.

Away from the café he stopped and looked uneasily all

around him. Then he homed in on the back of a man who was examining paintings of seascapes in an art gallery window; this perhaps was the man he sought. He was bald, like Saab man, but taller and thinner. Not the same person.

Somewhat reassured, he started back to the car. He looked down at his hands and saw they were shaking. When the shore breeze hit him on emerging from the back streets, he felt his t-shirt damp and ice-like against the small of his back. Then he once more froze in his tracks and stared across the street. There was no sign of Judith and the children. The car had disappeared.

Fourteen

IN PARIS, ALL THOSE YEARS BACK, he had shared an apartment with a French student who was studying Japanese and doing a dissertation on the works of Yukio Mishima. Henri also considered himself a fine sabreur and had tried to teach Thomas how to fence.

This latter detail ended up putting a severe strain on their relationship.

Henri was a refined, almost effete, Frenchman and he came from a well-heeled family; he would frequently refer to himself as 'très dix-septième'. Hence, perhaps, the epées and fencing and the intention one day to visit the Archibald Harrison Corble Collection, located in the library of Louvain University, Belgium.

After much cajoling from Henri, Thomas had finally

conceded and agreed to a few basic lessons in use of the foil. These took place in a local gymnasium; just the two of them, Henri bringing along with him a borrowed face-mask for himself. His protective tunic and mask he gave to Thomas and proceeded to introduce him to the rudiments. It all went wrong, the second lesson.

Henri took too readily to the role of master of fence. To illustrate how poor his pupil's parries and defence were he jabbed and prodded Thomas forcibly in the chest. Despite the padded jacket, that evening Thomas noted with alarm the cluster of blue-bruised spots dotted on his chest; these he probed gingerly with his fingers. When Henri continued in this corrective vein, the second lesson, Thomas exploded.

— Bastard!, he suddenly roared in English from behind the mask.

Henri had just executed a particularly aggressive Italian thrust, stabbing the capped epée into Thomas's sternum. People sharing the gym stopped and looked around. Henri stopped and straightened up and stared. Then he moved suddenly when Thomas tore off the face-mask and flung it at him with force. Next, he cast aside his sword and lunged at Henri with his fists. As Henri fled for the changing rooms, Thomas tried to aim a boot at his white-clad backside but was held back by a bearded man who had been shadow-boxing nearby.

This show of pique strained relations for the next couple of days until the evening Henri arrived into the Café Irlandais in Place Contrescarpe, pale and in a state of shock.

— You look like you've seen a ghost, Thomas said, suddenly concerned.

There is a scene in Sam Peckinpah's *The Getaway* where Steve McQueen is at the counter of an electrical shop and behind the salesman is a whole bank of TV sets, all on. Suddenly, unbeknownst to the shop assistant, McQueen's mug shot appears on the full array of screens as he is a wanted bank robber on the run. Something similar had occurred to Henri, not his face but that belonging to one of his Japanese student acquaintances.

Henri had been shopping in Boulevard Haussman and passing one of the big department stores located there, Printemps or Galerie Lafayette, had glanced at a window display full of TVs, when the Japanese student's face flashed suddenly up on all the screens. Although still a student he was also a recognised authority on the works of Ryunosuke Akutagawa and was frequently invited to give talks at international conferences; he had also murdered his German girlfriend and served portions of her up to friends for dinner. Thomas knew that Henri had visited the student's accommodation on at least two occasions.

— But not for dinner, he had blurted out. Right? I mean you didn't ...

And then he decided it would be more useful to go and pour Henri a stiff drink.

Steve McQueen himself died that period, and John Wayne; and John Lennon was shot in New York; and, at home, the hunger strikers began, in the May- time, with Bobby Sands.

But it was the Japanese student that came to mind as Thomas stood frozen on the seafront of Les Sables d'Olonne; and the killer on the ship out, and the melée in Belvès. Then suddenly his wife pulled up beside him in the car making him step back sharply from the kerb. She let down the driver's window and stared at him.

— Good God, she said, alarmed. What's the matter with you? You look like you've seen a ghost.

Fifteen

— I SAW YOU COMING AND THAT family wanted a parking space so I pulled out to let them have it. I went and turned at the roundabout, she explained.

— Did you not see us waving at you, Dad? Molly added.

— You looked like you were in a wee world of your own, Laura stated.

— Shift over. I'll drive, he said.

— Calm down, Thomas, Judith urged. Is there something wrong?

— Yes, Dad, Laura interposed. Take a chill pill, will you.

— Quiet Laura, Judith advised.

Thomas glared at his eldest daughter in the rear view mirror.

— Nothing's wrong, he said, but in a tight-lipped fashion. I just got a bit of shock when I saw the car was gone. That's all.

In silence, they left Les Sables d'Olonnes. Judith switched on the sound system and the Willard Grant Conspiracy was one of that day's chosen bands. Thomas, however, turned the player off.

— I've got a bit of a headache, he said.

Judith turned in the passenger seat and studied his profile with concern.

— Are you sure you're all right? She reached across and felt his forehead.

— I'm just tired, he assured her.

— Well. Let's go back to the campsite. The kids can go to the pool before it closes and you can have a lie-down. How does that sound, children?

The kids in the back all cheered, but in a muted fashion, in deference to their father's mood. However, Thomas was already indicating to pull across traffic into the large Carrefour on the outskirts of the town.

— I thought we needed some shopping? he said by way of explaining the detour.

— We do; but we can get away with putting it off 'til tomorrow, Judith said.

— The pool'll be closed, Jason protested.

— We'll just be a' minute, Thomas insisted. It'll be a quick shop. You lot don't even need to get out.

By the time he had parked, Thomas had revised this last suggestion. Now he insisted that they all go into the supermarket.

— That way, he justified his edict, it'll speed things up.

— The pool's still going to be closed, one of the kids muttered.

As they trailed behind, just out of earshot, Judith lightly touched Thomas' arm and said:

— You're acting very strange, you know.

— It's nothing. I'll explain all later. Honest. I want to get the newspapers: check up on how old Lance Armstrong's doing.

— Okay, she conceded. But, if you ask me, you've been acting a bit strange all holiday.

— Wise up, he protested, reaching for a supermarket trolley and looking around to ensure that the children were following.

As the automatic doors wheezed open, they were hit by the artic blast exhaled by the refrigerated units containing a scree of shellfish. Aquariums snorkelled as they passed and there were glittering displays of astounded fish on ice trays. The kids soon forgot their grumbling and they all stopped and ogled at the large, purple lingerie-like mass of inky squid, beneath the glass sneeze shield. The sickly sweet smell of ripening fruit also greeted them, set off somewhat by the sour, lactic aroma of the huge array of cheeses.

Judith stocked up on oeufs plein air, beurrier doux, emmental rapé, lardons, terrine de campagne, biftecks, fruit and cheese and Yoplait yoghurts. Thomas went in search of the Librairie.

He bought all the main national newspapers and as many regional ones as he could find. On his way to the counter, he stopped and went back to the display racks and picked up a copy of L'Equipe. Next, he purchased two bottles of red wine and a twelve-pack of Kronenburg.

The swimming pool at the campsite was still open by the time they got back. The kids wriggled into their damp swim wear and were off for the final half-hour before la fermeture.

Thomas set the charcoal and got it lit; he uncapped a Kronenburg, poured Judith a wine. He had managed to put off discussion of his mood until a more appropriate time, although still insisting there was nothing to talk about. Instead he sat down and went through the papers. Nowhere did he find reference to a jail-break in the Dordogne nor any journalistic condemnation of a flawed legal system responsible for allowing the early release of a suspected serial rapist. Saab-man was still locked up somewhere and not stalking the streets of Les Sables D'Olonnes. He sat there and felt relieved; and stupid.

71

Out of the corner of his eye, he watched the corners of the charcoal whiten. The smoke smelt good in the warm evening air. He took a long swallow of beer and turned to the actual stories in the paper he had open on his lap. Despite the warm evening, he shivered to discover that it was thirty-one years to the day since the Manson murders. He did not appreciate the coincidence.

That night, before falling asleep, Thomas got out of bed and double-checked that the door and windows of the mobile home were securely locked.

Sixteen

THERE WAS AN ARTIST PAINTING AT a table behind them where they sat, at the Café de la Paix, in the little square of St. Hilaire de Riez. Jason and Molly flanked the man who sat with a glass of beer and a box of paints and was daubing onto an artist's pad. His burly left arm acted as an easel.

— Ça vous dérange pas? Thomas enquired pointing at his children.

The bearded man responded more with a facial moue and a shrug of his massive, bear-like shoulders and it was evident he was amused by their curiosity and attention.

Thomas turned back in his seat and regarded the square.

— Continue, his wife commanded for he had at last agreed to open up to her. He had particularly done so when she had declared to him:

— There's times when it just doesn't feel like a holiday. It feels more like we're on the run.

In the Good Friday Agreement, between the Government of the United Kingdom of Great Britain and Northern Ireland and the Government of Ireland, there was a five point section on Prisoners. Point number one stated:

' Both Governments will put in place mechanisms to provide for an accelerated programme for the release of prisoners, including transferred prisoners, convicted of scheduled offences ... '

There had been a killer on board their boat, as they left the port of Belfast; a notorious beneficiary of this early release scheme. Thomas remembered seeing passengers take gradual cognisance of the man's presence among them, picking him out, although his time in prison had slimmed him down; he was no longer the bulky, overweight gun-man captured on television, firing into the crowd of marchers and pitching grenades which would kill three bystanders. No-one pointed; rather there were nudges and nods of heads in his direction where he sat in bikers' garb with a young woman beside him in similar attire.

— Didn't he take up sculpture or something? Judith asked. And find God, to boot.

— That's right, Thomas affirmed, looking around to check again on the two youngest children; Laura was indoors watching local youths play babyfoot. He was probably going over to attend an exhibition of his stuff, he went on.

Thomas sat silent for a moment and Judith allowed him to and made no comment. Instead she reached for her coffee and took a sip of it.

— It's just that holidays are supposed to be getting away from it all. Aren't they? And yet there he was: hijacking the holiday. It wasn't even the first day of the holiday: it was the first fucking hour.

— There were people like him released on all sides, Judith reminded him.

— I know. I know, Thomas assured her. But seeing a psycho like that before you've even left the country, when you're supposed to be going off and relaxing and enjoying yourself: it sort of makes a mockery of it.

— You don't know that he's a psycho, she put in.

— I know what I saw on T.V. And I know what went through my head later that night, out on deck.

Here Judith looked at him, a little startled. His face was grim as he returned her look.

— It was one of those times I went out to stretch my legs. Get a breath of fresh air. I was standing at the back of the ship, on the lower deck, back from the rail. It was dark and we were well out in the Channel. You could see the lights of other ships bobbing in the dark, way off in the distance. And the next minute: out he comes and he comes and stands at the rail, right in front of me. He didn't see me, but I knew it was him: I could see his profile as he came out of the light, the pony-tail and hawk nose. And he's standing there, oblivious to me and there's nobody else around-

— You're not going to tell me you were thinking of ... She didn't finish her sentence but continued to stare at her husband.

— For a split second, I was. For a split second, I imagined him disappearing into the tonnes of white water the Seacat spews out its rear end; I saw him sinking like a stone. Now: what way's that to start your summer holiday?

The couple sat once more in silence, for a while; but she was to rouse herself and speak again. Before this, she absent-mindedly watched a young priest emerge into the sun-flooded square from the dark interior of the church which comprised one side of the square; he carried a motorbike helmet in his hand.

— You wouldn't hurt a fly, she declared at last. Oh I know you've a temper on you; but you rarely show it. Not like me. I'm always flying off the handle.

Thomas shrugged and reached forward for his glass of beer.

— In any case you need to get over it. Her voice had grown sterner. For all you know maybe he has changed his ways; maybe he regrets his past actions. We've all got to move on. And, what's more, things have improved.

— I just don't trust peace. It's like the Holy Grail.

— Well, you bloody well better start trusting it. This holiday is beginning to cost a lot of money and you're not going to spoil it brooding half the time. Just take a look around you. It's beautiful.

And, as if he needed the assistance, she proceeded to describe the scene: the young priest hiking up his soutane now in order to get onto his moped, a group of gendarmes, looking like they'd just knocked off, in their short sleeves with their kepis in hand laughing and having a bit of craic; the children watching a Monet lookalike who kept dipping his paintbrush into his beer.

— Let's just enjoy ourselves, she concluded.

— What gendarmes? Thomas asked, looking around him.

His children were suddenly at his side, waving two of the café's napkins in his face.

— Look what that man drew for us, Molly whispered eagerly.

They were the briefest of brush-strokes, but somehow, in the midst of the swirl of arabesques and curlicues, something of each child's character had been captured and made discernible.

— Did you say 'merci', Thomas enquired twisting around in his seat.

The artist was already on his feet, his materials tucked under his arm. Despite his bulk, he was nimbly negotiating the labyrinth of tables and sun-shades and making for the square. Thomas called out his thanks.

— De rien, monsieur/dame, he replied to both of them, turning to face them. They could see multi-hued streaks and stains of paint through his beard. As he turned to go he paused and said:

— Et. Bonnes vacances.

Then off he ambled, bear-like, across the square, to disappear into the shade of an alleyway opposite.

Seventeen

THEY DID NOT GO BACK THEN, immediately, to the campsite. They dined out on seafood, (the children had chicken and chips) and then drove to La Plage des Mouettes. THE STONE ROSES were singing 'Bye, Bye Badman' on cassette, as they pulled into the parking lot, overlooking the sea.

Like the drizzled paint streaks on 'Monet's' beard, the sinking sun leaked a palette of hues onto the surface of the high tide and the soft swell smeared and suffused it through the water. La haute marée left a narrow band of sand and couples, young and old, and solitary dog-walkers strolled its length.

It took but a moment's contemplation of the scene for the two of them to exchange enquiring glances and for Judith to call the children and canvas their opinion:

— What do you children say to a night time swim?

Dusk was slowly dislodging daylight from the beach but it was still quite bright and the sky was clear, turning a dark, burnt blue. Perhaps they realised the later than usual hour, but the children cheered the proposal and Thomas pulled the beach bag from the boot of the car. The evening was mild and the damp, grainey swim-wear no great discomfort.

Some promenaders, in jumpers and fleece-tops, stopped and stood and spectated as the family immersed itself in the neon-like sea and Thomas took the plunge first and he swam underwater for a while before surfacing and being dazzled by the huge, molten shield, balanced on its edge on the horizon. He bobbed on the gentle swell and blinked his eyes and saw a sailboat still out some distance from the shore. The children kicked and flailed past him becoming silhouetted and seal-like as he watched. Judith surfaced beside him and got her arms around him.

— This is brilliant, she said.

— Magic.

He dived under once more and conjured up swirling sand clouds from the sea-bed and when he surfaced it was suddenly darker and the sky was splashed with stars. The sun had set leaving a soft, lemon-yellow bruising in its wake. Judith was already on the beach, calling the children to come out. He swam to the shallows and rolled himself out of the water, just another tumbled Gulliver on the shore; and he lay a while like that looking at the stars. Then he shivered and got up and joined the others fumbling into their clothes. The vestige of light still clinging to the air did not bother them and they dressed quickly, unembarrassed by any brief nakedness, as people strolled nonchalantly by.

Though they showered afterwards, they could still taste traces of the sea on each other as they made love. The children were asleep and Judith had at first snuggled in close to her husband under the sheet, and moments later he had arched his back slightly and she knew she had his attention.

Afterwards, he lay awake, listening to Judith breathing deeply as she slept, finding it difficult himself to fall asleep as it kept coming back to him how he had not told the full truth of events on board the boat, that first evening out.

Eighteen

THEY RACED EASTWARDS THEN, IN the mad zigzag of their itinerary, to get to Nîmes and the final campsite, located out in the Ardèche countryside; flashing past furnace blasts of fields of sunflowers and the sun-warmed faces of churches, worn and ancient and Molly piped up, at one point, from the back seat:

'Now that we're in France, does that mean God speaks French?' and they splashed through heat mirages shimmering on the roads and manoeuvred through small, tightly streeted towns, such as Marennes, which would widen suddenly into great spaces given over to squares and market stalls, stopping for croque monsieurs and crèpes, sucre/beurre, the children marvelling at caged birds and chickens and rabbits and Judith forbidding Thomas to reveal the eventual fates of the fowl and game as they strolled to stretch their legs before beginning again, rolling past farm-houses now with sun-coloured masonry and red tiles, traversing an array of rivers, through toll booths; Judith and Thomas sharing the driving, Thomas spotting one house from a bridge with a balcony built out over the river, imagining what it would be like to sit there, eat meals there, work there; listening to the likes of Interpol and Joy Zipper and the air conditioning on all the time now, for the weather in the south had been so hot and the woodland and brush so dry, the Fourteenth of July fireworks had been cancelled except that one day it rained and the baked ground was unable to absorb the deluge and a torrent of water had flushed through the campsite so that when the ceramic earth at last relented , cars and vans became mired and stuck and static in the cloying red-clayed muck and mud.

This campsite's shop was run and ruled by Mme. Cerbère. She struck terror in the hearts of Dutch housewives and Belgian husbands, anyone who could not speak French and were unacquainted with the ways of the shop. Laura, Molly and Jason refused to go to the shop for bread in the morning. Judith did too. Laura had run foul of her on the first day when she had lifted a bar of Swiss chocolate off a shelf to study the wrapper.

— Doing, dad, what you're always on at me about: improving my French and then suddenly she's shouting at me and pointing at the shelf. 'Keep your purple hair on, missus,' I sez to her.

— In French? Thomas asked.

You could spot new arrivals by the transgressions they perpetrated. Thomas felt sorry for a young English woman who attempted to lift two croissants from the baker's basket to the left of the till, just by madame's customary perch at the entrance.

— T'as pas reservé? Madame shouted at the woman. She looked up in startled fashion and all in the queue behind her felt sympathy for her but no-one attempted to explain that, whereas baguettes were readily available, if you wanted the likes of a croissant or pain au chocolat, brioche or pain aux raisins, these had to be ordered the previous day and a 'ticket' dispatched by Mme Cerbère. Instead, everyone shifted a little uneasily and pretended to read the headlines of the Dutch or Belgian or English or French newspaper that they were purchasing that morning.

— Her bark's worse than her bite, Thomas tried to assure Judith and the children.

Although she made no concession to anyone's lack of French, she did not just reserve this 'bark' for tourists; locals experienced it too. On one morning, Thomas witnessed the delivery of huge, fragrant barrels of baguettes; he even helped the lady van-driver in with them. Mme. Cerbère frowned at the batch and, looking closely at them, remarked:

— Elles sont bien cuites, quand-mème.

— Non, The girl sounded hurt and lifted a least brittle one out as if to disprove madame's assertion. Unimpressed, she said:

— Ce n'est pas 'Raffarin', quand même.

An obviously politicised Mme Cerbère was here referring to the decree passed in 1995 by the Minister of Commerce, Jean-Pierre Raffarin, which granted artisinal bakers proper legal representation.

The decree was amended in 98 and stated that it was against the law for a 'boulangerie' sign to be displayed on an establishment except where professional bakers had been 'personally involved in the kneading of the dough, its fermentation and its shaping.'

The way was thus opened for the generation of retro-innovators such as Lionel Poilâne, Eric Kayser and Dominique Saibron. They were determined to develop new ways of baking bread in the old tradition; re-inventing slow-rise versions of baquettes, boules and batards.

Mme Cerbère was evidently not including the lady van driver in with this esteemed company; either that or she was just loath to 'remercier son boulanger'.

However, by dint of using his French, Thomas had

gradually befriended Mme. Cerbère. It began with his conscious decision to greet her in the morning with the rather formal, almost school— textbook formula:

— Bonjour Madame. Comment allez vous?

She had stopped in the midst of her fussing and bustling and looked at him for a moment before stating that she was well and enquiring after his own health.

The next day he discussed the weather; the next, he pronounced ' À demain' with a southern twang, adding a 'g' sound at the end and her features would soften whenever, after this, he entered the shop. On one occasion, just before the midday closure of the shop, he happened upon her, sitting on the stoop just outside the shop. The heat was intense, the sunlight dripping down through the thick, protective foliage of the chestnut trees that lined that part of the site. Thomas was making his way slowly to the pool. Spying Mme Cerbère sitting in the shade, he spoke, with what he hoped was enough irony to show that he knew he was stating the obvious:

— Il fait chaud.

She looked up at him and smiled, revealing a line of sharp, irregular teeth.

— Ah, monsieur, she shouted. Vous savez: c'est les canicules.

More, even, than in the Dordogne, they went river swimming. They purchased elasticated swim shoes, to enable them to stumble over sun-scorched rocks and boulders and hot sand shoals, to plunge into the fresh clear river water. They made up a game called 'crocodile', where Thomas chased them underwater and the kids, and on occasions Judith, screamed and waded and floundered out of his reach. Jason lost his left shoe.

On two occasions, they swam at the Vallon Pont d'Arc. They accessed one small river beach by a sharp descent from a crowded carpark above. The opposite bank seemed inaccessible except by water and they all swam across and scrambled onto huge slabs and shelves of rock and basked there a while in the strong sunlight. On the return stretch, canoes appeared around the bend but the current was slow and they had no difficulty swimming between them. In the heat, the river levels were low and they spoke to one family in the campsite who told of having to drag their canoes from one pocket of water across parched bed to the next stretch of water.

Back on the river bank, an elderly couple had moved into the space next to where they had spread out their blankets and towels and bags. The two of them reclined on white, plastic sun loungers, the type you find beside swimming pools, and Thomas wondered how they had got them down the sharp incline. The woman was in her late sixties and she sat back, topless in the sun and it all felt natural and fine and Thomas lay back and closed his eyes, relaxing, he felt, at last. The caves had been closed to the public but, as he lay there in the simmering sunlight, he fancied he could feel the energy of the parietal drawings from the Chauvet Caves pulse through the layers of limestone to him like ancient ley lines. Moments later, he had to open his eyes again and look again at the great, natural arch that gave the place its name, sculptured into the limestone by the river. He half-raised his neck to survey too the sheer sides of the canyon; then he lay back and dozed.

However, the river was high, their second visit there, the water agitated with great cuts of current in its fast moving surface. It was the day after the downpour. They sanctioned the children to remain in the shallows and swam themselves out into the middle. It was only then they realised the flow was full of floating tree debris and storm flotsam; when the sodden carcass of some bird spun swiftly past her face on the turn-table of the current, Judith lost her stroke and her head went under and she came up choking and spewing water. Thomas helped to steady her; the river seemed to snap and suck around them. Suddenly a canoe shot around the bend and narrowly missed

Thomas's head. There was a wide-eyed child in the front of it and a man, sweating and toiling with his paddle in the stern. He shouted something back at them but it was lost in the rush of the water and the river skirled the green craft on downstream. When they got back to the river beach, they realised they were clabbered in green weed fronds, leaves and algae. They peeled these off like stickers, or children's transfers.

They were still picking pieces out of their hair, on the terrasse of the café they favoured in Barzac. Barzac had become another Belvès for them: a mazey hill-top town to stop at on the way back to the campsite after a day's outing. The children had quickly acquainted themselves with the whereabouts of the freezer for the ice-cream.

A Cork man, sitting at a table adjacent to them, spoke up:

— I couldn't help overhearing, he said. But, if you haven't been entirely put off swimming, I can recommend the most remarkable place.

— That would be great, Thomas assured him. Would you like to join us?

— You're fine, the Cork man declined. My own family's due along any minute. But, if you're into swimming, you've got to go to the Cascades of Saudadet. Don't ask me to spell it but it's marked on the local tourist information map.

The man's family appeared down the street and turned out to be his wife accompanied by three, tall, grown-up sons. They had all come away together on holiday. One son took an order and disappeared into the dark interior of the café, and the other two, at their father's request, assured Thomas and Judith that the cascades were a truly awesome place to swim.

— As long as there's no dead wild-life floating about, Judith said ruefully.

— Well, to be fair: there is a sign warning that so many people have drowned there, the other son said. Eighteen, I think. But don't let that put you off.

Nineteen

— IT SAYS HERE, THE CASCADES GOT their name from a combination of 'Saut' and 'Hades', Thomas informed his wife.

— Hades as in Hades? Judith asked.

— And 'Saut' as in leap or jump.

— It still sounds like a great place to swim.

In the event, they did not make it. The last day in the campsite coincided with Laura's birthday and it was her treat to go instead to the town of Uzès for a shopping trip.

Thomas lasted the pace as far as La Place aux Herbes where, spying tables and chairs set out under an inviting awning, he informed them that this is where they would all meet up in an hour's time. The others took off up a narrow, arcaded street and Thomas browsed in Le Parefeuille book store located just off the square. He purchased the most recent Philip Djian, a

Yasmina Khandra and, out of respect for the recently deceased Jean-Claude Izzo, a copy of La Marseillaise newspaper.

This he was reading at one of the outdoor tables when Judith and the children reappeared from another of the little streets that issued into the square. They were carrying bags of varying sizes. When Thomas had ordered drinks for everyone, he informed them:

— Andre Gide used to come here for his summer holidays.

Unimpressed by this piece of information his eldest daughter said:

— Do you want to see what I bought, dad? And proceeded to pull out garments from the bags and hold them up against herself for Thomas's approval.

Brendan Behan had once burst into his father's pub, on a bleak, blustery November's day, decked out, his father said, in a shiny, new, yellow Sou'western. He had just disembarked in the town, from off a coal boat in the docks.

— How did you know it was Brendan Behan? Thomas's brother had once asked.

— You just knew, their father assured them. Anyway, a few drinks down him and he stood and announced as much to all and sundry.

It seems he was much taken with the clientele, in particular the Spike Davis who was much given to reciting large swathes of Robert Service at great length. Behan insisted on buying him drink even though the Spike, unusually, owned up to his own impecunious state and inability, therefore, to reciprocate.

At one point, in these proceedings, Behan came away from the crowd that had assembled around him and beckoned Thomas's father to a quiet side of the mahogany counter. Behan, it seemed, addressed him as 'sir'.

— Sir, he enquired. Would there be a pawnbrokers or some such similar establishment in the town?

The pub was located opposite the town market and adjacent to this was McManus's Pawn Shop. Thomas's father informed Behan of as much and Behan disappeared.

Thomas and his brother would listen in awe to the tale of this encounter and the subsequent one in Dublin; but their father read mostly thrillers, especially by Leslie Charteris and he was unimpressed by his illustrious customer. However, he did once concede that, for those minutes of Behan's absence, the bar seemed to pause, to lower some of its hue. Then Behan reappeared in his shirt sleeves, bursting back in out of the November murk minus the yellow Sou'western, but with the ring of money in his pockets.

— He recited some stuff, their father recollected. And later, sang some songs. Republican to start with.

Then, just as the songs were beginning to change from green to blue, some client suggested a change of venue and Behan and his new-found friends went off into the night.

— Thank God, their father would say. By that stage, I was sore tempted to bar him. Your mother was upstairs, for God's sake.

A couple of years later, Thomas's mother and father went to Dublin and while she shopped, his father stepped in through the side entrance of a bar in Abbey Street. It was an L-shaped counter with a partition hiding the longer expanse and no sooner had he ordered his stout than he heard the distinctive and familiar voice. He stuck his head briefly around the corner of the partition and there swayed Behan, holding court.

— Did you not join him? Thomas had once mischievously enquired.

His father had gazed at him and his brother all the time shaking his head slowly.

— That eejit? He, at length, replied.

What he did was drain his pint and leave. He went to find a quiet bar for a peaceful drink. He was not a bookish man and, in any case, preferred 'The Saint'.

In Place Aux Herbes, in Uzès, Thomas sat and made admiring comments, concealing all the while, his sudden shock at how grown up his daughter had become. Then Jason suddenly shouted out:

— Look. There's that man from Dublin.

Somewhat shocked, Thomas looked all around him.

— Where? Judith said, shielding her eyes with one hand from the glare of the sun and scanning the square.

— Not here, Jason said. In the paper.

He was pointing at a group photograph in La Marseillaise which lay folded inside out on the table. They all studied the grainy image closely. It comprised the organising committee and guests of a festival of music and culture in the town of Guincamp. Standing to the extreme right of the group, grinning at the camera, was a dead-ringer for Nial, the Dubliner.

— I thought you said he'd gone home, Judith enquired.

— He did. That's not him, Thomas declared.

— It looks like him, Laura stated.

— Maybe it's part of his charity work, Judith said.

— You've all had too much sun, Thomas maintained as the waiter arrived with a tray of drinks. And, what's more, he said to his wife. It's your shout.

They had booked an early evening table at the campsite restaurant, in order to celebrate Laura's birthday. Earlier, Judith had smuggled a cake into the premises.

The birthday girl beamed and blushed in equal measure after the waiters had emerged, on tip-toe, from the kitchen, only to burst into song, one of them holding the cake aloft, with sparklers fizzing from it, and people in the restaurant sang along and clapped time and in the end applauded and congratulated her.

— Has it been a good birthday? Judith was anxious to know, once all the excitement had subsided.

— Yes, Laura replied. But I miss not having my friends.

— That's one of the drawbacks with having a birthday during the holidays.

— Try having your birthday at Christmas, Thomas complained.

— What sign are you? Molly enquired.

— Sagittarius, Thomas replied.

— Not you. I meant Laura

— A Leo, Laura answered.

— Which means the lion, Judith explained.

— And I'm a centaur, Thomas added.

— Big deal, Jason said. It's Laura's birthday. We're not interested in yours. No offence.

Judith put her arm around her husband.

— Aw. Poor Dad, she consoled.

Thomas put on a pained look and said:

— I'm wounded.

After the meal, they allowed the children to run around to the bar area where there was a D-J and various musical entertainments. Thomas and Judith strolled to the tree-lined avenue area of the campsite, festooned with strings of outdoor lights, an arena, that night, for a boules championship. Thomas stopped by one of the marroniers and studied the play. Christophe, one of the camp entertainers and organisers of events such as this one, spotted his interest and came across to him. He had half an idea that Thomas spoke French and in a mixture of English and French, asked him if he wanted to join in: there were three French people wanting to enter but they lacked the fourth competitor to make up the numbers. Thomas faltered a moment and looked at Judith.

— Go ahead, she urged.

— Mais, j'ai pas des boules, Thomas put it to Christophe.

— Pas un problème, Christophe beamed, slapping Thomas on the back. He disappeared only to return moments later with a set of silver, polished boules.

Having only ever watched the sport from a distance, Thomas was fascinated to be let into the rubric and stratagems of the game. He had never before realised that each game was up to thirteen. Some of the players had retractable, magnet-tipped rods with which to pick up each boule, avoiding thus the need to bend down.

To begin with, his marksmanship was poor.

— You are not throwing missiles, one of the players advised him.

Then one of his opponents kindly demonstrated for him a better technique. Holding the boule by the merest tips of his fingers, he brought his arm up in a smooth and fluid movement at the apex of which he released the boule and it sailed in a graceful arc through the air. There was a satisfying thud as it hit the soft earth and it rolled back briefly to snuggle up against the jack.

— Tu vois, he said, turning to Thomas. C'est plutôt un mouvement de douceur.

Twenty

THEY BROKE THE LONG TREK HOMEWARDS by stopping at the Hotel Central, adjacent to Le Grand Temple in Nîmes. This was a friendly, family run establishment but without a lift. As Judith wanted the luggage with them, in the room overnight, Thomas twice trudged upstairs for two flights, lugging their two heavy suitcases up to the large family room that had been reserved for them. Molly bounded up and down the stairs with him while the rest lounged on the beds in the hotel room. Laura had opened the shutters and the windows and they were enjoying the fresh breeze that blew through from the narrow side-street below.

The whole family was tired. They had risen early to clean the mobile home intending to get on the road early enough to give them time to get to and explore the city. The children had requested, in particular, a visit to the Roman amphitheatre. However, they had miscalculated the volume of French vehicles heading for the coast and had crawled a lot of the way in the slow-moving, stifling tail-backs, Thomas intermittently trying to interpret the messages coming from the Bison Futé.

Thomas let the second heavy suitcase drop with a thud and regarded those who were stretched out on the beds.

— Pass your father a bottle of water, Judith told Jason.

As if in reaction to this idea, Thomas raised both his arms in the air to reveal two great Africa-shaped maps of sweat at each arm-pit.

— Stinking, Laura proclaimed.

— Have a quick wash, Judith said, getting to her feet. Though, I'm afraid there's no shower. You better hurry before the Colosseum closes. I'll hoke out a clean shirt for you.

— You spoil me, Thomas said as he disappeared into the bathroom.

The woman at the reception took a map of the town from a wooden rack behind her and helpfully threaded a line in red ink through the zig-zag of narrow back streets to help them arrive at the Boulevard des Arènes.

Their way took them past the Hotel Lisita at the restaurant of which Thomas had hoped they might dine that evening; the place, however, was closed.

— That's where the matadors stay, he said to the children.

He stood on tiptoes at one of the windows and tried to peer through his reflection to get some impression of the dark interior. As he did so, the others wandered on only to come out suddenly and stop and stare up at the impressive façade of the first century amphitheatre where their father's bullfights still took place.

— Come on, Jason hastened forward. We've got to see inside.

— Watch the traffic, Judith shouted after him.

They had to queue for twenty minutes, standing then shuffling forward under the arcaded, ancient exterior. They shivered a little in this shade and it was cool too when they eventually got into the network of corridors, up out of which they climbed to emerge onto the circular ranks of tiered seating of the spherical arena.

— Let the games commence, Thomas said, gazing all around, trying to take it all in.

As they clambered up the terracing, he pointed out to Judith:

— Look: there's not one pillar or stanchion to obscure your view.

— Wouldn't want to miss a disembowelling or anything.

The two of them stopped to catch their breaths and look down again at the arena below. A stage structure was being dismantled, scaffolding loosened and lowered to the ground, shirtless workers in hard hats scuttling around.

— There must have been a concert, Thomas said. I think Radiohead played here last month.

Judith looked up and away from the arena and suddenly gripped Thomas by the arm.

— Oh my God, she exclaimed. Look.

Thomas looked around in the direction of her startled gaze. High up, at the uppermost rim of the colosseum stood Molly, her frail form in stark outline against the bright azure of the sky. They could see her long hair blow about her in the wind.

— I'll get her, Thomas said, starting forward.

— Don't startle her.

All the time resisting the urge to shout to her, Thomas scrambled up the steep seating; even wearing shorts and trainers he found it hard going scaling the huge hewn squares of rock that separated him from his youngest daughter where she stood close to the edge, unperturbed by the sheer drop before her. She had obviously made the ascent in no time at all.

Ken Kesey came to Belfast in the August of 1999. He was on a quest, touring, in a replica of the original day-glo school bus, sites of mystical significance. His quest was not so much the Grail as Merlin and he and his band of 'Merry Pranksters' were due to visit the Giant's Causeway and look for Merlin there.

They were also performing a musical spectacle in Belfast, complete with a 'thunder box', bizarre costumes and Neal Cassady's son John on lead guitar. The afternoon of the performance, Thomas took the children down to the Limelight, the downtown venue for the extravaganza, and he got himself and the children photographed along side the manic schoolbus. It still said 'Further' on the front. On the half-chance, he ushered the children into the Limelight, through the stage doors. He had a copy of 'Demon Box' with him but there was no sign of Kesey. Instead, however, one of the pranksters appeared and spotting the children she came over to them. As they chatted away, this beautiful woman mentioned their intention to visit, the following day, the Causeway and Jason and Molly promptly regaled her with stories of their own visit there just days before. This was the first time both Thomas and Judith realised Molly's mountaineering skills as she had skipped swiftly up the basalt steps and columns of solidified lava.

— She's like a mountain goat, Thomas had boasted to the Merry Prankster.

This memory came back to him now with force as he grazed one of his knees. He slowed down as he drew close to her.

— Molly? He said softly. Come on away from that edge now. He could hear sirens and klaxons coming up from the busy traffic below, circulating the arena.

He stretched out a hand to his daughter.

— Come on, he said again.

— I'm alright, dad, she insisted. I'm not a child you know. She shuffled closer to the edge.

— I know you're not, Thomas hastened to assure her. But you know how nervous I get; and that wind's very strong.

He kept his hand outstretched though it wavered slightly in the wind.

— Alright then, she consented and moving away from the edge she allowed Thomas to take her hand in his and then he had her securely enfolded in his arms. As he stood with her like that, only then did he take in the view that had obviously captivated his daughter; the breezy vista of red rooftops, shelving off into the blue distance, the dizzy swirl of traffic on the Boulevard de la Liberation.

— It's beautiful, isn't it? Molly said to him.

On hot days such as this, there are outdoor air-conditioning units, balanced on long spindly tripods, positioned on the terrace of the Café de la Grande Bourse. At intervals, these gasp out clouds of frozen vapour that disperse around the heads of the customers sitting at the tables there. From their table, Judith gazed up at the edifice of the amphitheatre.

— It is very impressive, he said to her.

— It's still hard to reconcile it with its history of bloodshed.

— Do you know that every time a death sentence is commuted, anywhere in the world, they turn the floodlights on in the Colosseum in Rome?

— Is that true?

— I believe so.

— Well, Judith considered. There's hope for us all yet.

In Ken Kesey's absence, the Merry Prankster offered to sign his book for him back that time in Belfast. 'Lovingly w/peace', she wrote, signing it: ' Anonymous'. On their way back out the stage door, she kissed the children on their foreheads and Thomas on the lips.

Twenty-One

— PLEASE. JUDITH REPEATED HER REQUEST IN a low but insistent tone, so as not to alarm the children, half asleep in the back of the car. However, Laura picked up on it and said:

— What's the matter?

— Nothing, Thomas said; and then, to his wife: You're crediting them with being semi-literate.

— I'm serious, Judith said.

They were on the last leg of their journey home. They had driven up the land-bridge route through England and having arrived outside Heysham with a few hours to spare, they had decided to drive on into Morecambe Bay, even though it was growing dark.

As they cruised along the seafront, Judith was convinced they had attracted the attention of a group of skinheads sitting on chrome garden chairs, outside a small café. She was adamant that at least one of the number had pointed after them. Thomas had checked in the rear and side mirrors for confirmation of any sudden interest in their passage but, although he could make out their pale, bald forms as they receded, he was aware of no unusual movement on their part. Nevertheless, he pulled over into a parking area and, switching Kasabian off, said:

— Well, I suppose we 'll be back in Belfast soon, anyway.

Telling the children to stay put, both he and Judith got out and went to the rear of the vehicle.

— Try it with your nails, he suggested.

It proved, however, to be a very aggressive adhesive and, at first, Judith only succeeded in scratching small striations across the face of the sticker.

— Don't mark the car, he said over her shoulder.

— You try, she said.

While Judith went and looked back up the sea-front, Thomas managed to claw at large sections and peel them off. Eventually, just a dirty, blackened oval of glue remained, with no letter decipherable on its surface.

— Come on. That's the best I can do. At this rate of knots, we'll miss the boat.

They got back in and Thomas swung the car around in the road.

— Do we have to go back this way? Judith enquired.

— Would you just calm down, Thomas said.

It was dark now and a cold breeze was blowing, but outside the café, Judith's skinhead sat in a tee-shirt with a crusader's cross on its front and stared at them and made some comment, for Thomas watched in the mirror as all heads turned and examined the car.

The traffic lights ahead of them turned red and, still in the mirror, Thomas watched as the St. George's Cross one and two others pushed themselves up out of their seats and started to walk towards them. He looked to see if his wife had noticed and surreptitiously, he reached forward and pushed the central lock button on the dash-board before returning his eyes to the mirror. Almost up to them, the amber light flashed and Thomas gunned the engine and sped off. The sudden acceleration made Judith look up and around her and they both saw the trio sprint into the street gesticulating and shouting abuse after them. In the glare of the headlights of an on-coming car, he noticed his knuckles were white where he held onto the steering wheel.

— Ladies and gentlemen, he announced suddenly to the car. I think it's time to go home.

— So much for the illiterate, she reproved him.

— Semi, he corrected her. I said semi-literate.

— I hope they can't fucking drive, she said.

Thomas laughed and looked in the rear-view mirror and accelerated, all at the same time, as Molly, in the back, alerted the others to the fact that mum had said the 'F' word.

Twenty-Two

INTO THE HOLLOW BELLY OF THE boat, they edged the car.
A deckhand, in bright, fluorescent overalls, made darting and
impatient gestures, insisting Thomas squeeze the car in beside a
touring van. Thomas had already taken the precaution of folding
the wing-mirror in, getting Judith to do the same, her side.

— Watch you don't bang the doors getting out, he said to the
children.

Thomas breathed it in, the air below-decks. Despite being a
noxious concoction of diesel and exhaust fumes, laced with sea-
salt, Thomas quite liked the smell. It made him think of
movement; travel; getting away.

— Come on you, his wife called back to him as she herded the
children through the close-packed vehicles towards the steep
stairs that would take them up to the lounge and seating areas.

Above, they rushed, Simpsonesque, to claim a table and seats and the children unloaded their gear: cards, books, paper and colouring pens. Judith sat back and unfolded the main part of the Observer newspaper. Thomas picked up the coloured sports magazine that accompanied that edition. He immediately turned to the lengthy article on Lance Armstrong.

Lance Armstrong had done it. Joining Miguel Indurain, Eddy Merckx, Bernard Hinault and Jacques Anquetil, he had just won the Tour de France for the fifth time. He had done it despite the many untoward incidents that had bedevilled that year's progress.

"There's been a lot of strange things that happened this Tour de France," he said at a press conference reported in the article. " And I need them to stop happening. It's just been a very odd, crisis filled Tour."

— I wonder if he'll go for a sixth. What about a magnificent seven? Thomas thought aloud; but then a huge shudder reverberated through the superstructure of the ship and the lit-up quay without seemed to shunt off suddenly like a train.

— We're moving, Jason declared.

It was only then that Thomas thought to look around him and survey the crowd. The boat was full of half-dead holidaymakers, on their way home, tired and jaded and giving in, at the last, to the whims and exigencies of importunate offspring. Exhausted adults draped themselves across benches and seats and looked stoical and morose. A few men swayed in the bar area, clutching plastic pint glasses of beer, determined to elicit the last ounce of vacation left them. Their laughter was too high, too raucous. Most would be back to work the following day. Thomas looked to the side, to what would be those seats equivalent to the ones occupied by the man and his companion that first day out of Belfast. Different people sat there now.

— I want something to eat, complained Molly. You said we'd get something to eat in that sea-side place and we didn't.

— Okay, okay, Judith conceded. What does everyone want? It can't be chips, mind, because you have to eat them in the restaurant and we'll lose our seats.

Eventually, after some negotiation, they settled for a mixture of cellophane wrapped sandwiches, crisps and soft drinks. After this, Laura leafed desultorily through a music magazine while Molly drowsed in her seat and Jason coloured in.

— When are we there? Laura suddenly piped up.

— About another hour, Thomas said, a response that drew a collective groan from the children. Laura flopped closed the magazine and leant her head against her mother's shoulder to doze.

Eventually, Thomas rose from his seat and went towards the door that led out onto the deck. As he emerged from the warm enclosure of the lounge area, he was buffeted once again by the cold, bluff breeze of the Irish Sea. Once again there was dark water all around, pierced through, here and there, by distant lights from buoys and beacons and from the heights and extremities of other maritime traffic. He stood, again, away from the rail, somewhat sheltered from the wind; and, once more, he thought of that first night at sea.

It had not happened as he had told it to his wife in the square of St. Hilaire de Riez.

There was a glass panel in the sliding door separating him from the interior of the lounge. He turned his head and looked now through the Perspex pane, as he had done then; for, from this vantage point, he had been able to peer in at the man sitting there with his female companion. Looking now, he realised suddenly what it was he had seen, what he had been privy to all this time and yet unaware of until that very moment.

He looked back out at sea. He moved over to the railing. He gazed down at the pale waves peeling off the side of the boat. Swaying slightly, he proceeded along the railing until he stood towards the rear, briefly oblivious to the 64 tonnes of violent, white water, hosing the boat back towards Belfast. The truth was: the man had never ventured out on deck; he had remained stuck to his seat for the duration of the crossing. His travel companion had run whatever errands had been necessary: food and refreshments. The man had, in fact, placed himself with his back to the sea, facing the boatload of people and had never once dared to go outside on deck. He had glanced once at the door with what Thomas now recognised as a startled, haggard look of agoraphobia. It was as if the image of the man was frozen now, for all time, in the frame of the door; paralysed and going nowhere.

Despite the wind and water, he heard his son's voice and turned around.

— Can I come out on deck? Jason shouted.

— Go and get a jumper first, Thomas called back. This isn't the South of France. You'll catch your death.

Moments later, his son returned, pulling a warm, yellow top on over his head.

— Hey! Lance Armstrong, Thomas reacted.

They stood together out of the wind and watched as the Seacat forged up the lough and the city began to appear, adrip with lights. Down through the droning decks, he felt the surge and voltage of water fusing into or blazing out from fjord and river mouth or threading through the delicate circuitry inland, of gullies and gorges, streams and rivers to burst back out again into larger water masses, lakes and loughs, seas and oceans, and channels such as this one which he felt himself and his family borne along upon and buoyant.

As they drew closer, Jason left his side and climbed up on the bottom rung of the railing. Thomas moved quickly to stand beside him. At one point, he stretched out his hand to take a hold of the yellow fleece and then stopped himself. He withdrew his hand and stood to one side, alert and watchful yet letting his son alone.

Looking over his son's head, he had difficulty making out the looming shapes of Goliath and Samson, the great yellow hurdles barely visible now in the dark. Instead, his attention was drawn to the bulbous, illuminated building Jason was pointing out to him.

— Look, his son called. It's the Odyssey.

A disembodied and metallic, megaphone voice announced then that it was time for passengers to return to their vehicles to prepare for disembarkation.

— Come on, Thomas said. That's us now.

They lingered, however, looking at this lit-up waterfront. Then, as they made their way through the throng of passengers, Thomas heard it for the first time: the new Babel of voices, accents and intonations, sailing with him into port; and then was when he knew he was nearly home.